Sports Illustrated KIDS
GRAPHIC NOVELS

STONE ARCH BOOKS
a capstone imprint

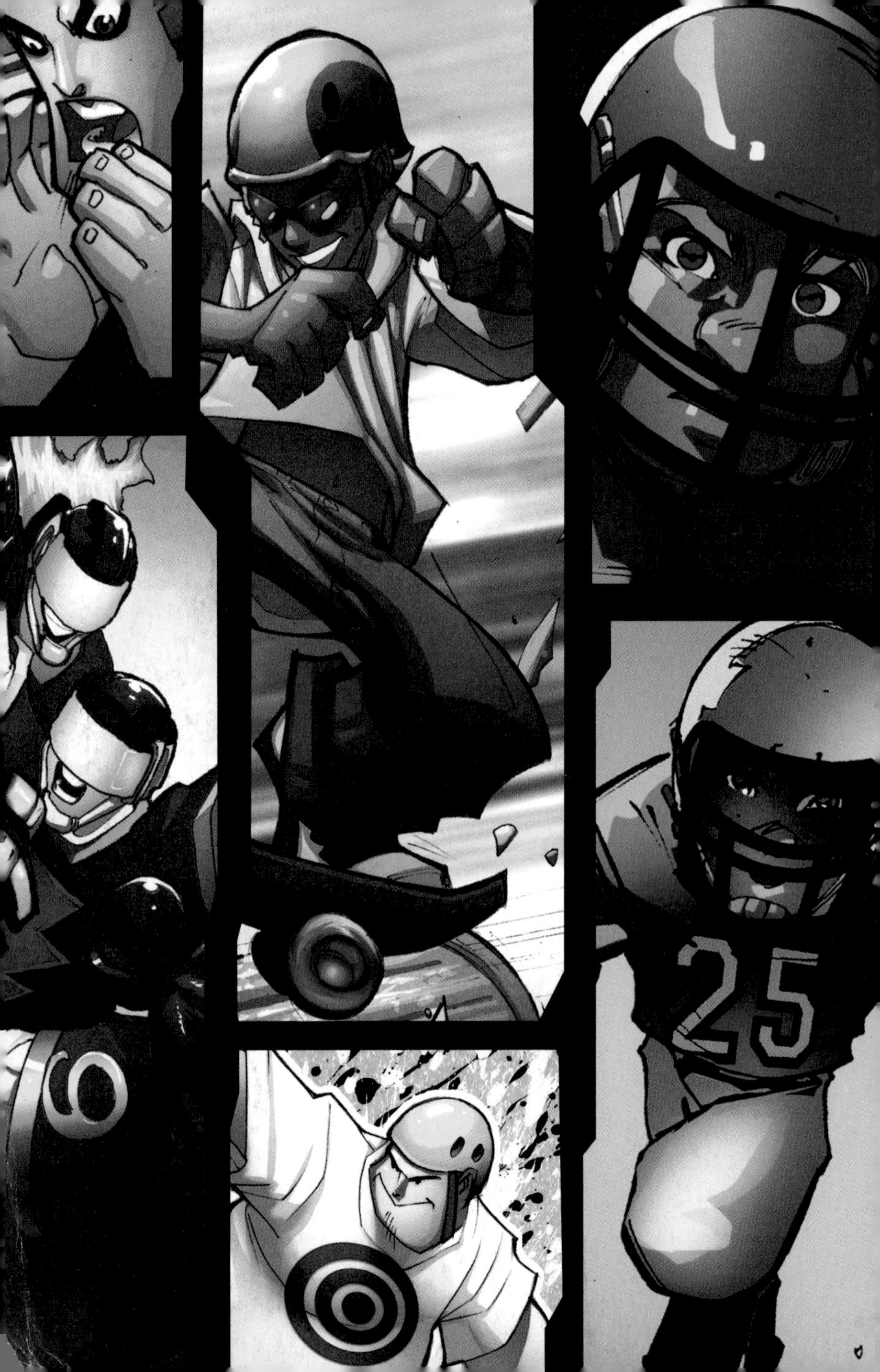

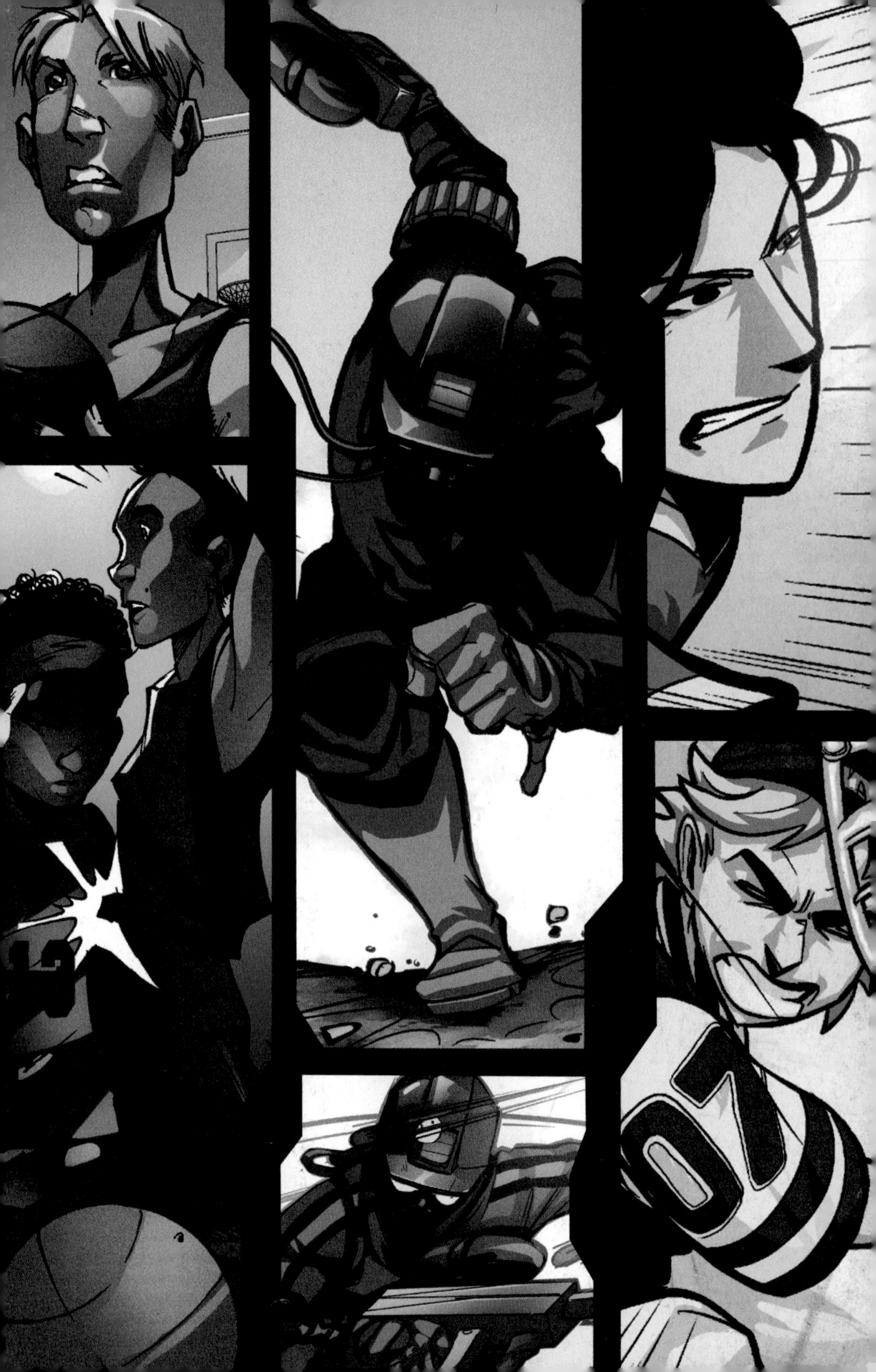

UP NEXT)))

on **Sports Illustrated KIDS**

:02 SPORTS ZONE SPECIAL REPORT

:04 FEATURE PRESENTATION:

SKATEBOARD SONAR

FOLLOWED BY:

:50 SPORTS ZONE
POSTGAME RECAP

:51 SPORTS ZONE
POSTGAME EXTRA

:52 SI KIDS INFO CENTER

BLIND SKATER LYONS FACES SIGHTED SUPER-SKATER THIS FRIDAY SIK TICKER

BLIND SKATER COMPETES FOR STREET COURSE TITLE!

MATTHEW LYONS

STATS:
NICKNAME: MATTY
AGE: 13
EVENT: STREET

BIO: Matty is blind, but you wouldn't know it by watching him skate — he has become a top-notch street course skater despite his disability. Matty has also developed a reputation as a local hero for his difficult grabs, stellar tricks, and positive attitude. Matty is almost always seen with his skateboard, and his best buddy, Ty, nearby.

Sports Illustrated KIDS

UP NEXT: SKATEBOARD SONAR

TYSON TAGGART

NICKNAME: TY
AGE: 13 EVENT: HALFPIPE
BIO: Ty is a hot-head who reigns supreme on the halfpipe. He skates hard and loves to put on a good show. Ty has been best friends with Matty Lyons since kindergarten.

BLZ vs BKS	3-1
TGR vs ROR	33-32
EAG vs BAN	14-7
SPA vs WLD	4-3
BAN vs ROR	21-15
RZR vs LIG	4-3
BLZ vs BKS	3-1

CLINTON WASHBURN

NICKNAME: CLINT AGE: 13 EVENT: HALFPIPE
BIO: Clint's a talented boarder who's trouble on — and off — the halfpipe. His best buddy is the big bully, Bing Hawtin.

WASHBURN

BINGLEY HAWTIN

NICKNAME: BING AGE: 14 EVENT: STREET
BIO: The only thing Bing likes to do more than pick on puny skaters is beat them senseless on the street course.

HAWTIN

JILLIAN SPEARS

NICKNAME: JILLY AGE: 17 JOB: PARK OWNER
BIO: Jilly's a true patron of the skating art. A talented skater herself, Jilly's park will host the All-City Skating Competition.

SPEARS

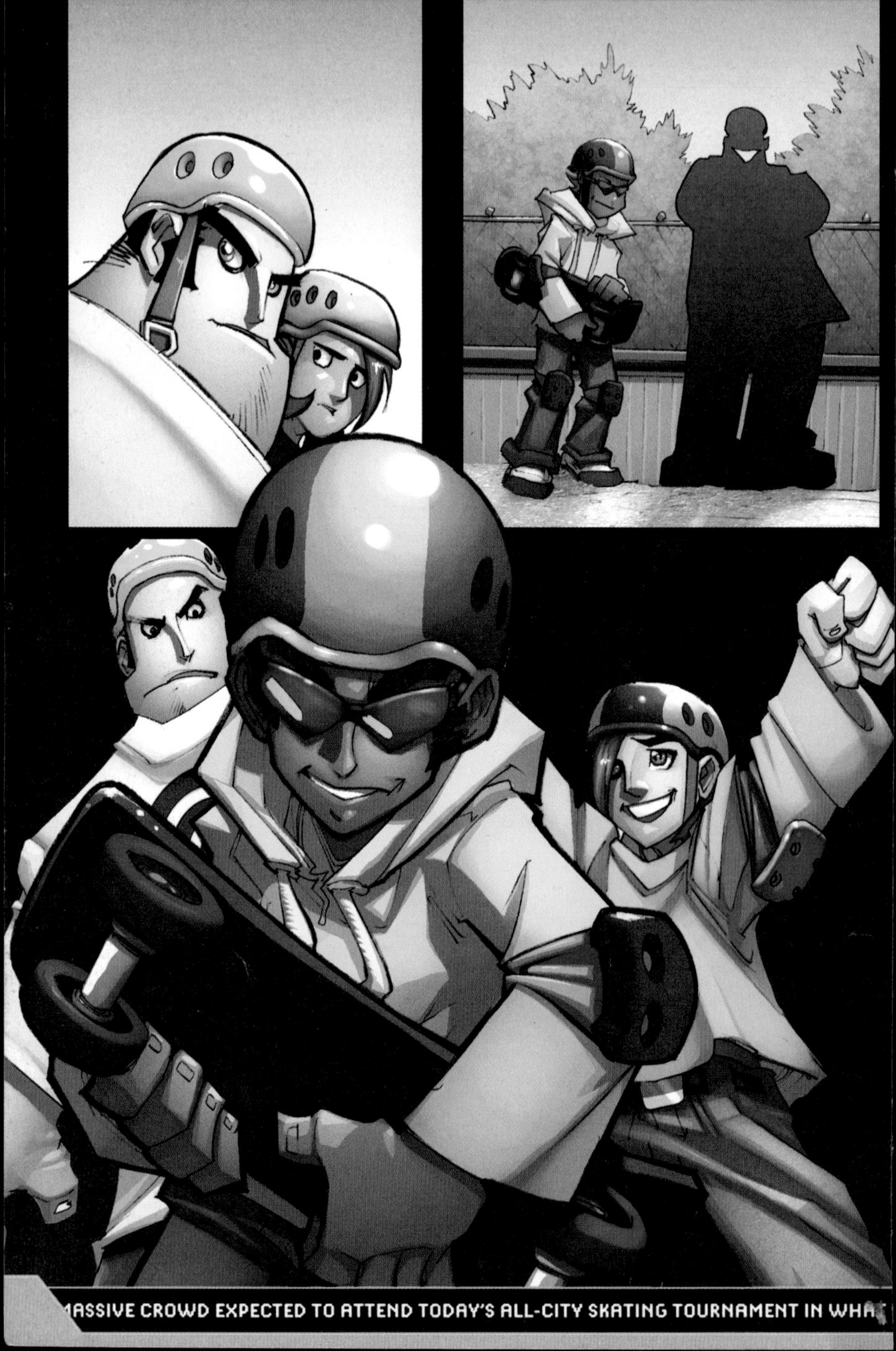

MASSIVE CROWD EXPECTED TO ATTEND TODAY'S ALL-CITY SKATING TOURNAMENT IN WHA

Sports Illustrated KIDS

PRESENTS

SKATEBOARD SONAR

A PRODUCTION OF

STONE ARCH BOOKS
a capstone imprint

written by Eric Stevens
illustrated by Gerardo Sandoval
colored by Benny Fuentes

designed and directed by Bob Lentz
edited by Sean Tulien
creative direction by Heather Kindseth
editorial direction by Michael Dahl

Sports Illustrated Kids *Skateboard Sonar* is published by Stone Arch Books,
151 Good Counsel Drive, P.O. Box 669, Mankato, Minnesota 56002.
www.capstonepub.com

Summary: Matty Lyons can do all the coolest tricks. His moves are even more impressive since he's blind. But not everyone is a fan of the talented grinder. During the state's biggest skating competition, former champion Bing Hawtin mocks Matty, saying that a blind kid has no chance to win. But Matty knows something Bing doesn't . . . seeing isn't everything.

Library of Congress Cataloging-in-Publication Data
Stevens, Eric.
Skateboard sonar / written by Eric Stevens ; illustrated by Gerardo Sandoval, illustrated by Benny Fuentes.
p. cm. -- (Sports Illustrated Kids graphic novels)
ISBN 978-1-4342-1910-7 (library binding) -- ISBN 978-1-4342-2295-4 (pbk.) 1. Graphic novels. [1. Graphic novels. 2. Skateboarding--Fiction. 3. Blind--Fiction. 4. People with disabilities--Fiction.]
I. Sandoval, Gerardo, ill. II. Fuentes, Benny, ill. III. Title.
PZ7.7.S79Sk 2010
741.5973--dc22 2009037870

Printed in the United States of America in Stevens Point, Wisconsin.
072010 005869R

OUBTEDLY BE A HEATED COMPETITION BETWEEN SEVERAL AMAZING LOCAL SKAT SIK TICKER

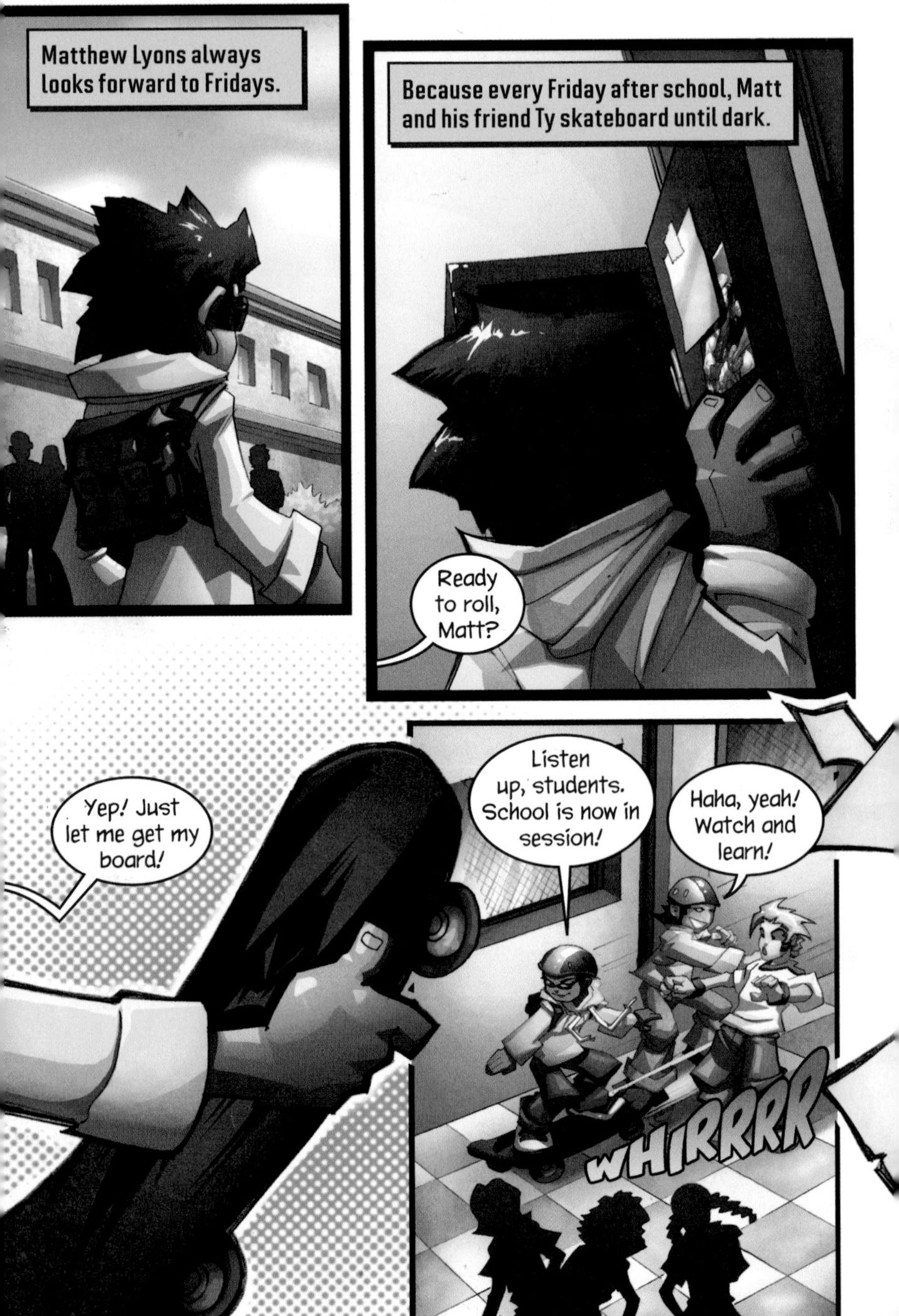

Matthew Lyons always looks forward to Fridays.
Because every Friday after school, Matt and his friend Ty skateboard until dark.
Ready to roll, Matt?
Yep! Just let me get my board!
Listen up, students. School is now in session!
Haha, yeah! Watch and learn!
WHIRRRR

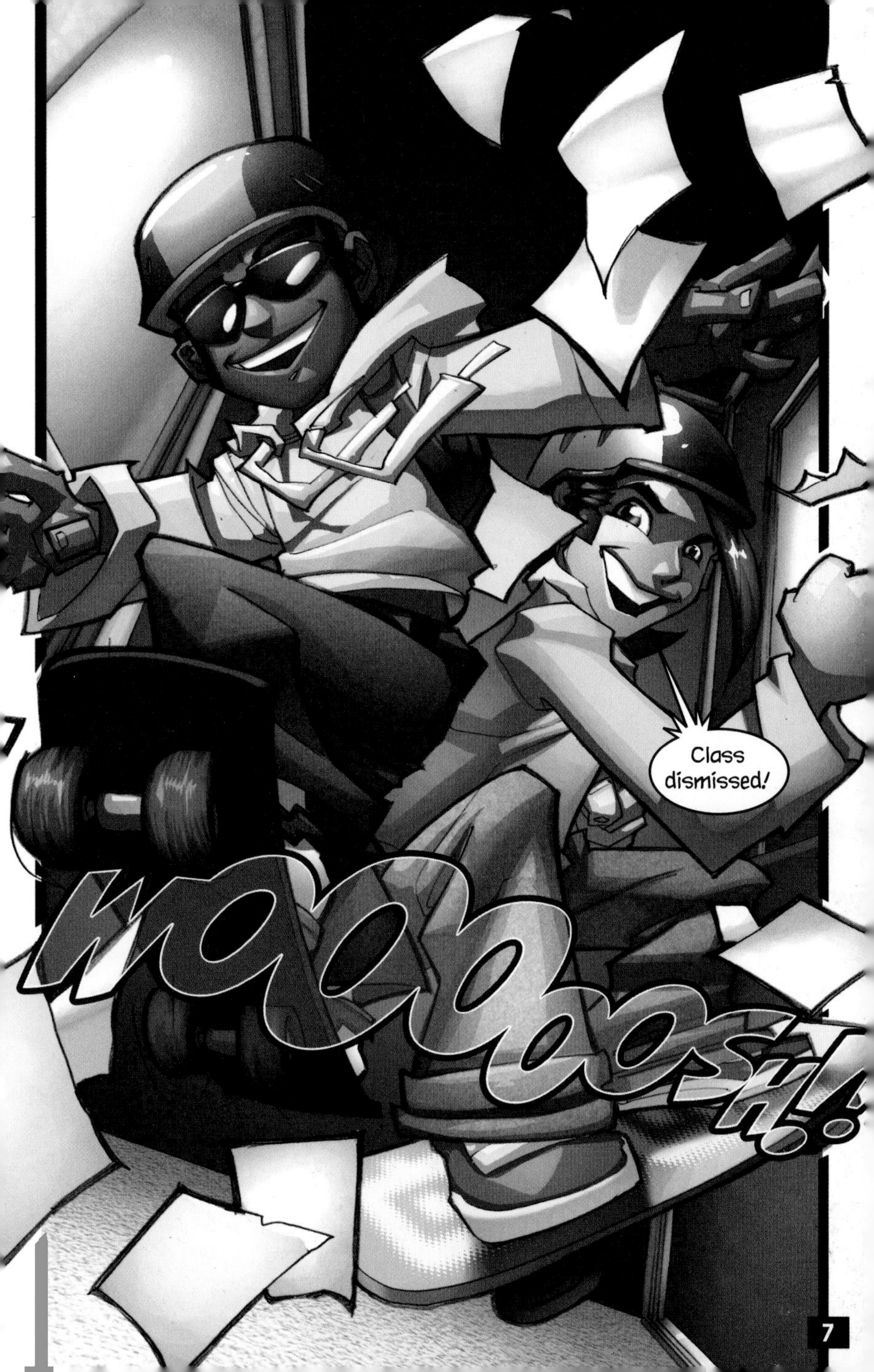
Class dismissed!
WHOOOOSH!!

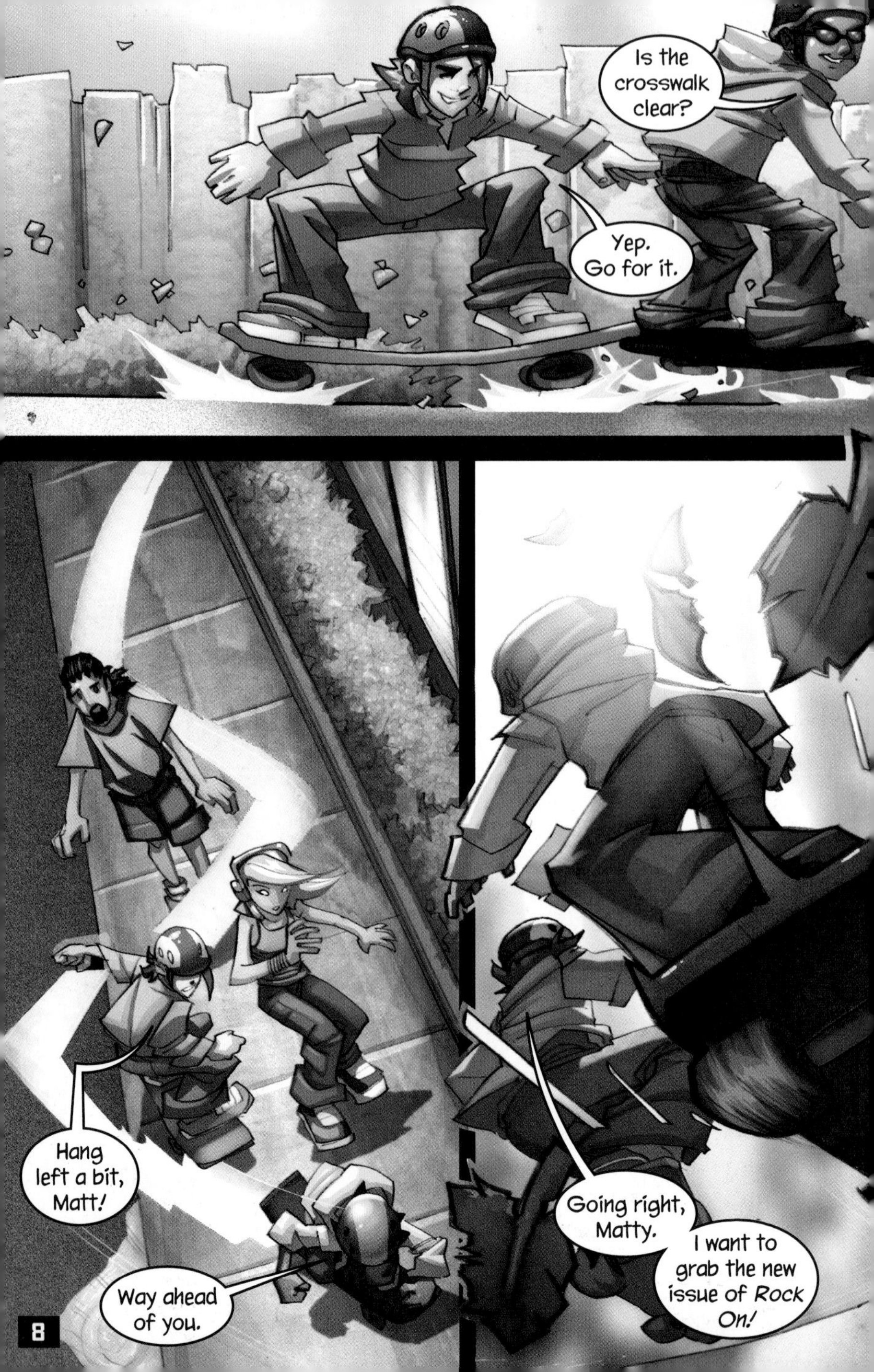
Is the crosswalk clear?
Yep. Go for it.
Hang left a bit, Matt!
Way ahead of you.
Going right, Matty.
I want to grab the new issue of *Rock On!*

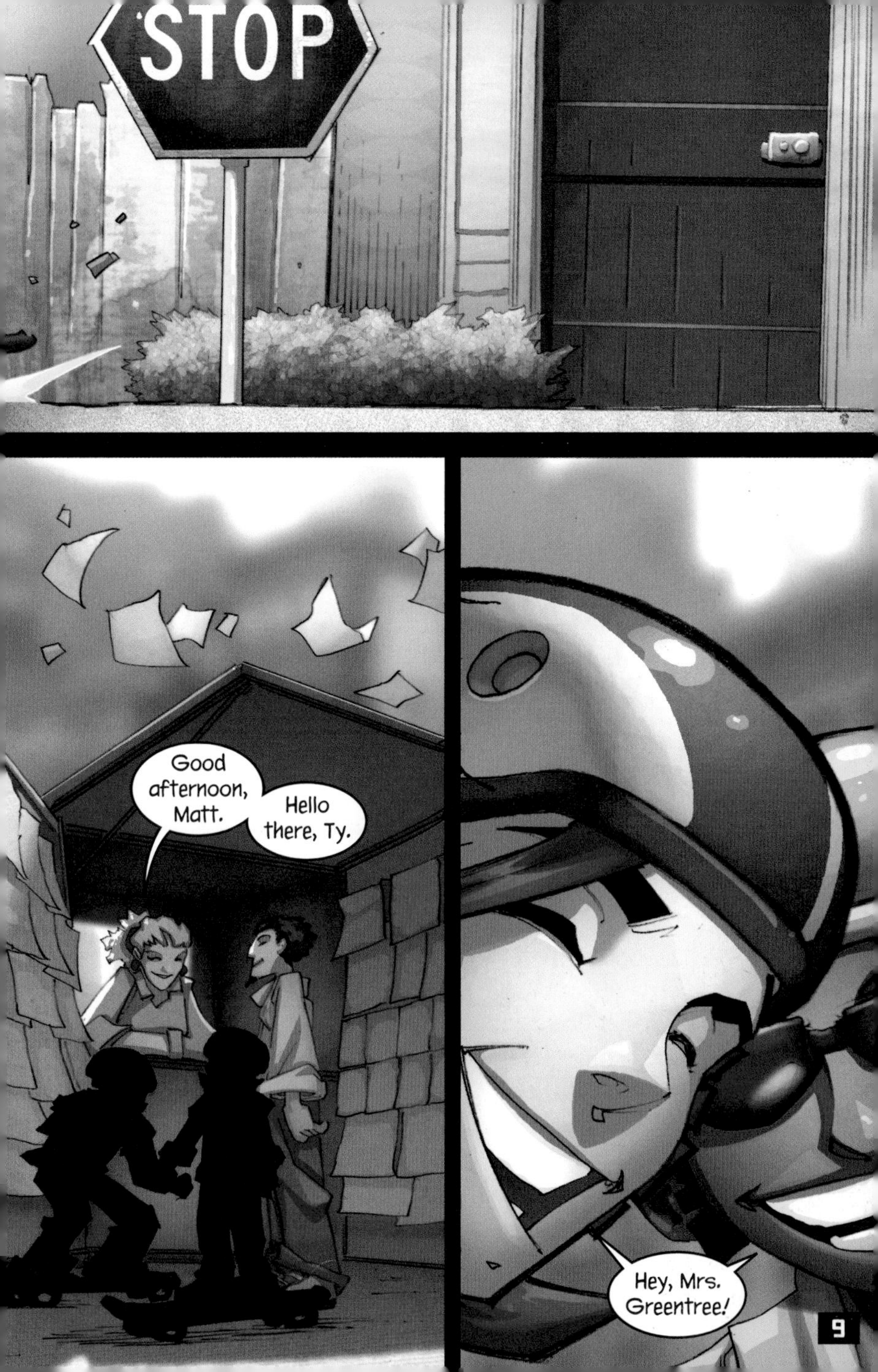
STOP
Good afternoon, Matt.
Hello there, Ty.
Hey, Mrs. Greentree!

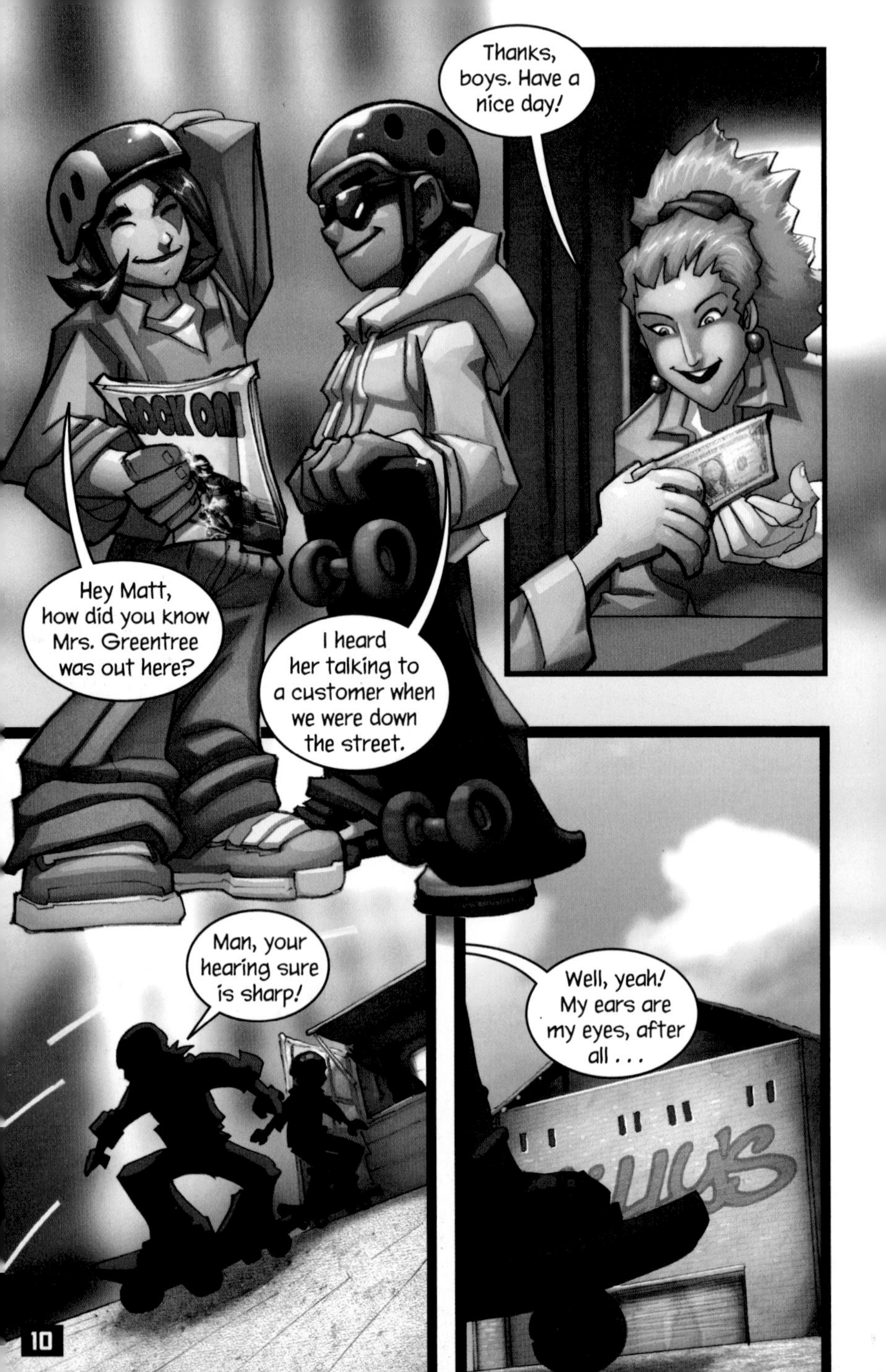
Thanks, boys. Have a nice day!
ROCK ON!
Hey Matt, how did you know Mrs. Greentree was out here?
I heard her talking to a customer when we were down the street.
Man, your hearing sure is sharp!
Well, yeah! My ears are my eyes, after all . . .

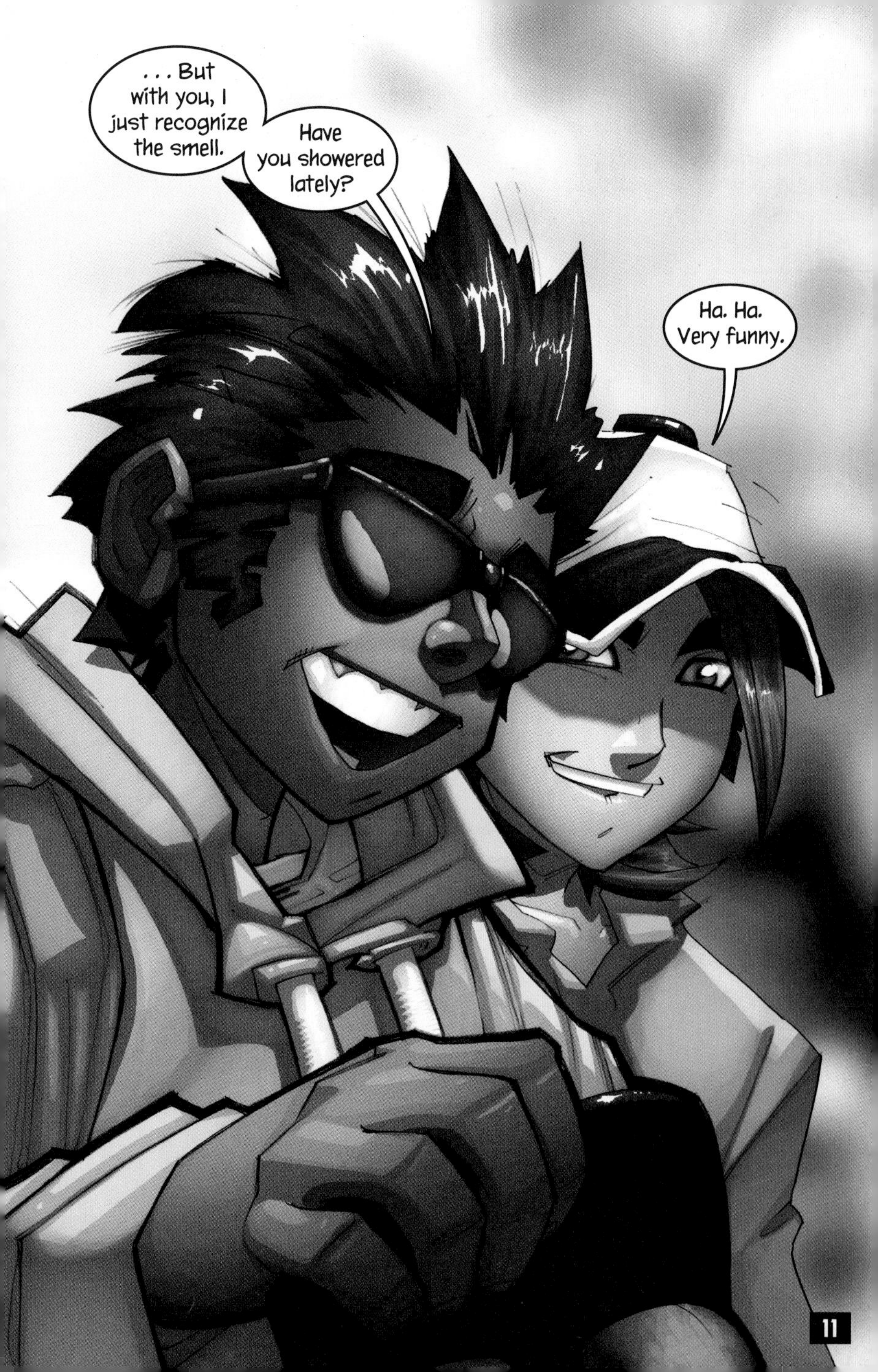
. . . But with you, I just recognize the smell.
Have you showered lately?
Ha. Ha. Very funny.

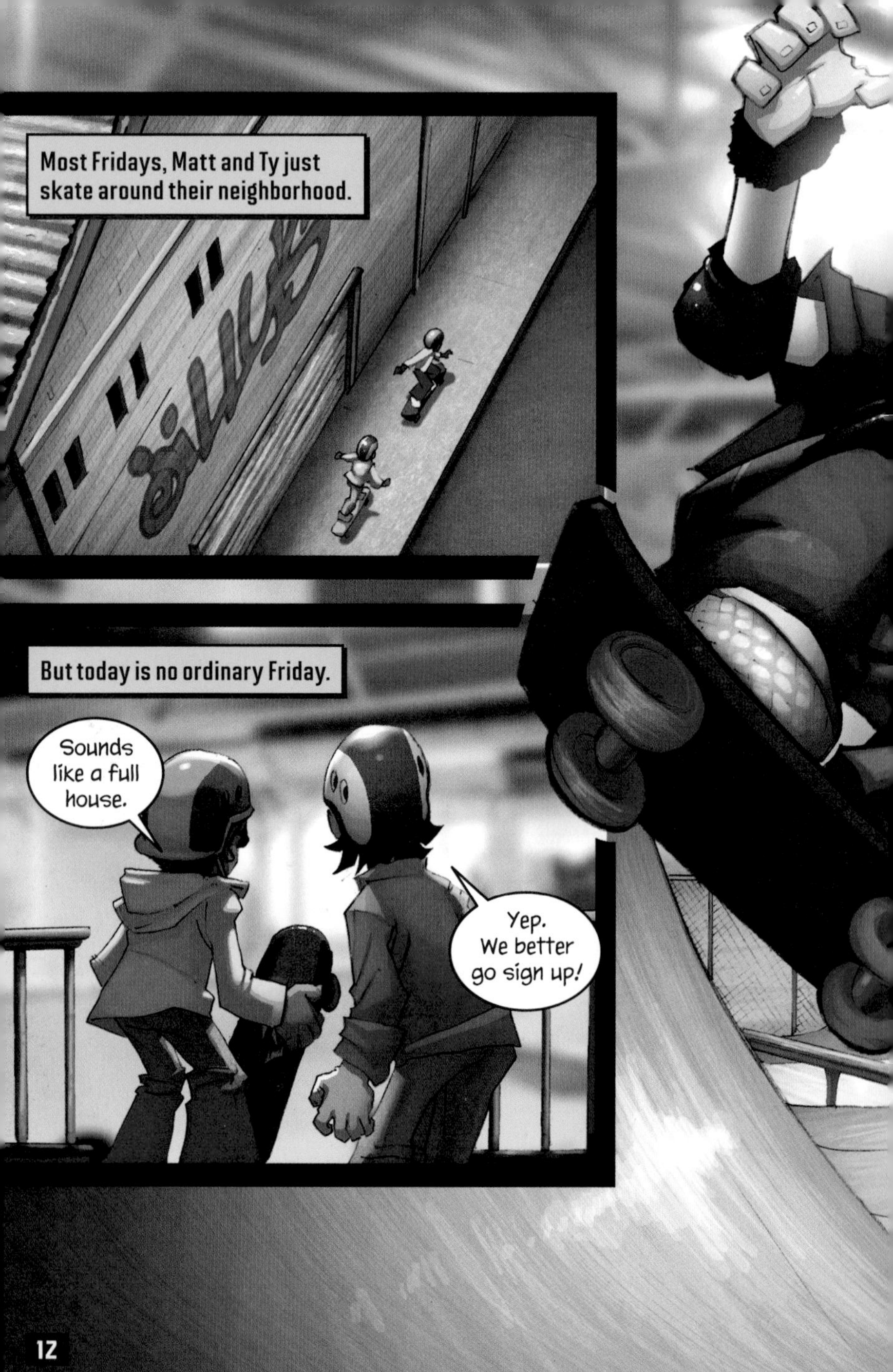
Most Fridays, Matt and Ty just skate around their neighborhood.
But today is no ordinary Friday.
Sounds like a full house.
Yep. We better go sign up!

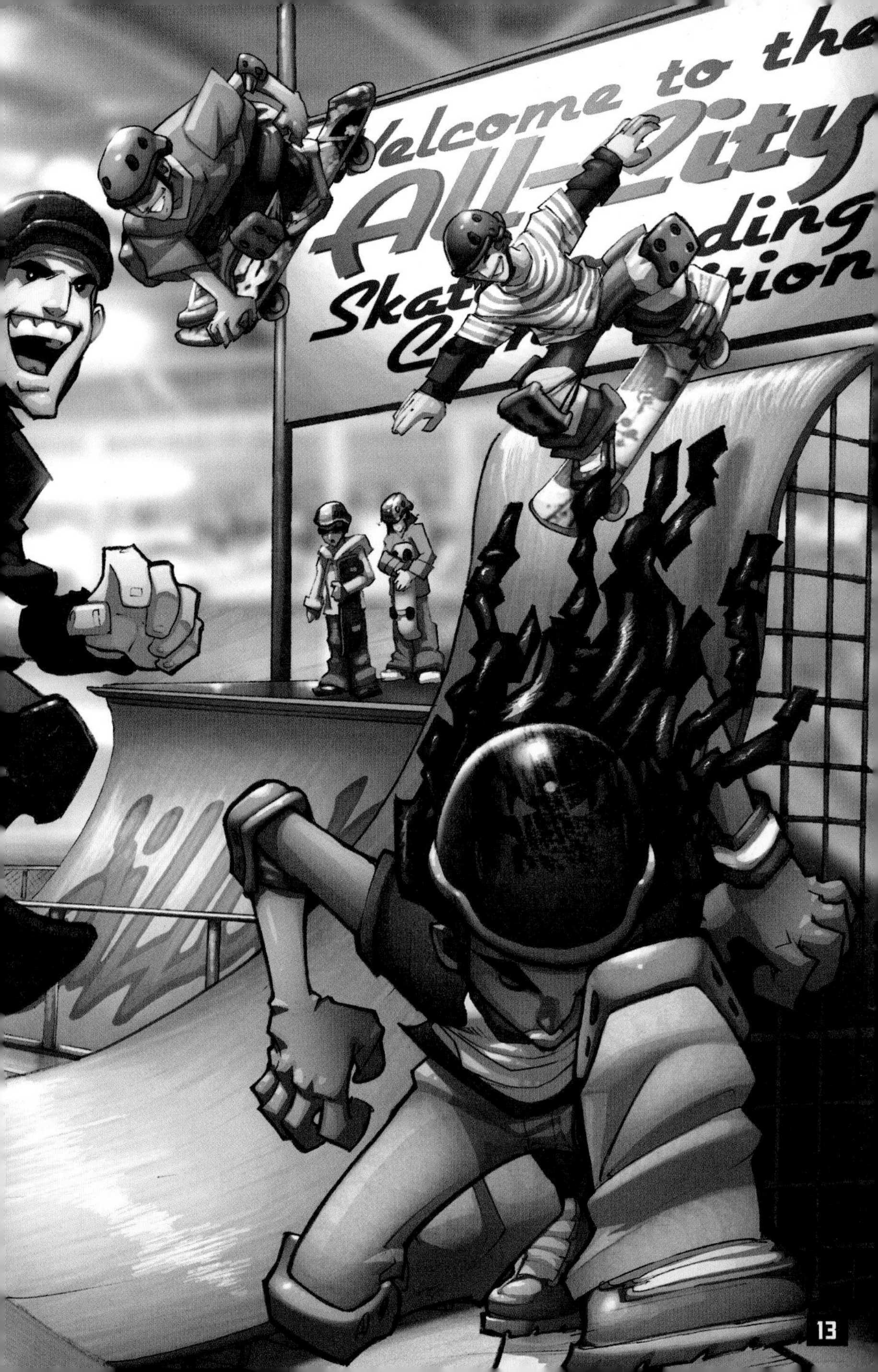
Welcome to the
All-City

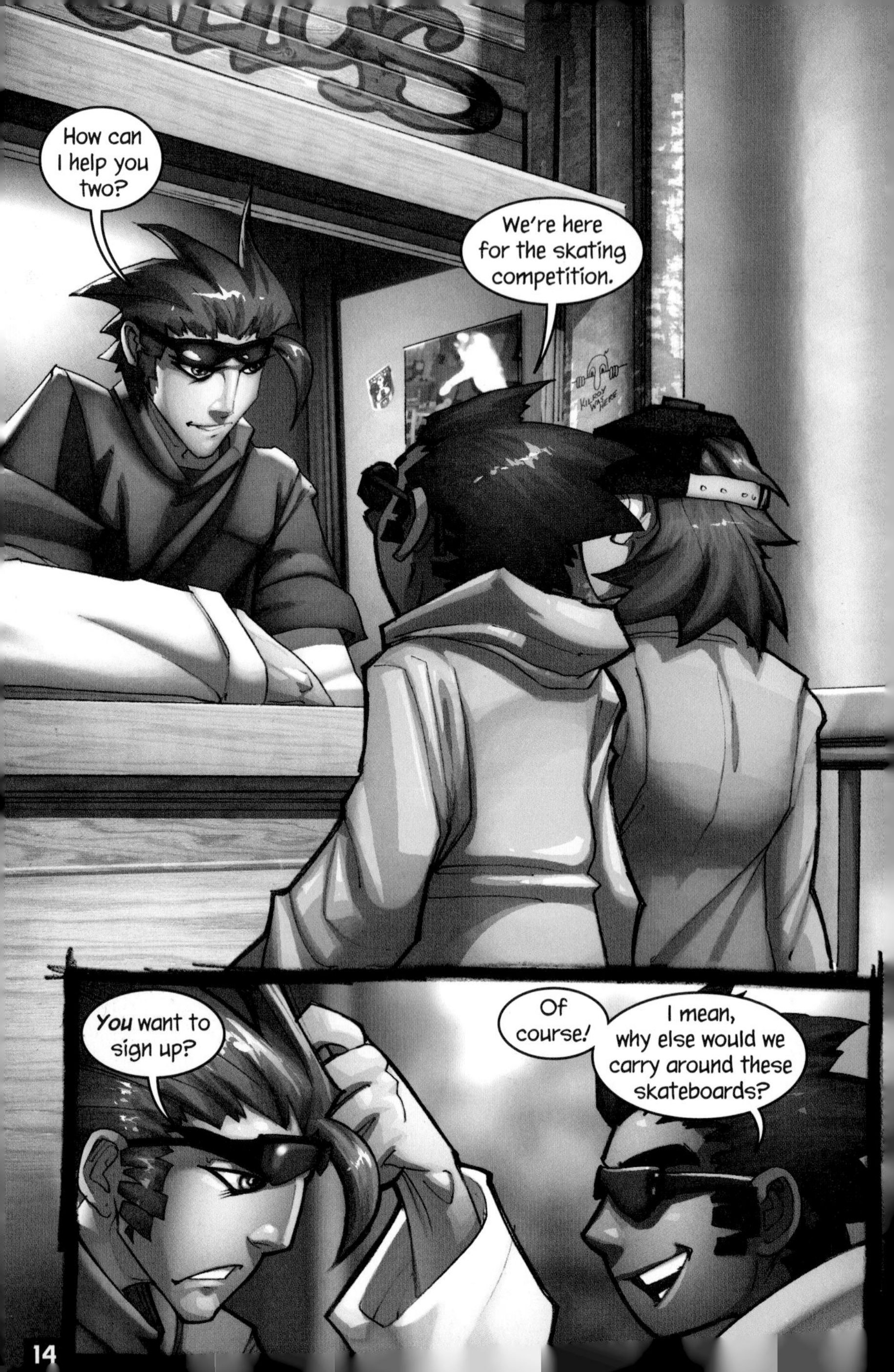
How can I help you two?
We're here for the skating competition.
KILROY WAS HERE
You want to sign up?
Of course!
I mean, why else would we carry around these skateboards?

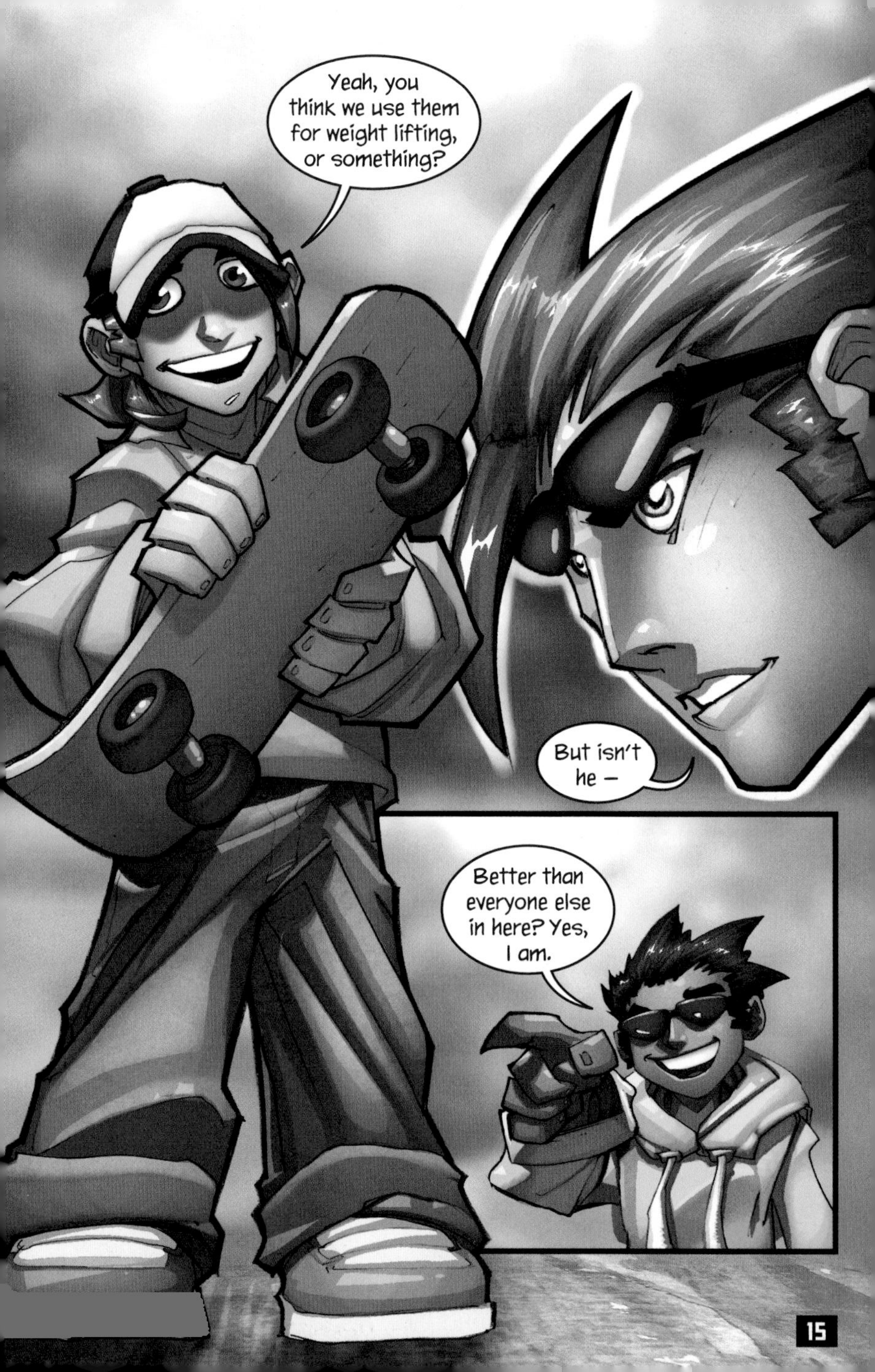
Yeah, you think we use them for weight lifting, or something?
But isn't he –
Better than everyone else in here? Yes, I am.

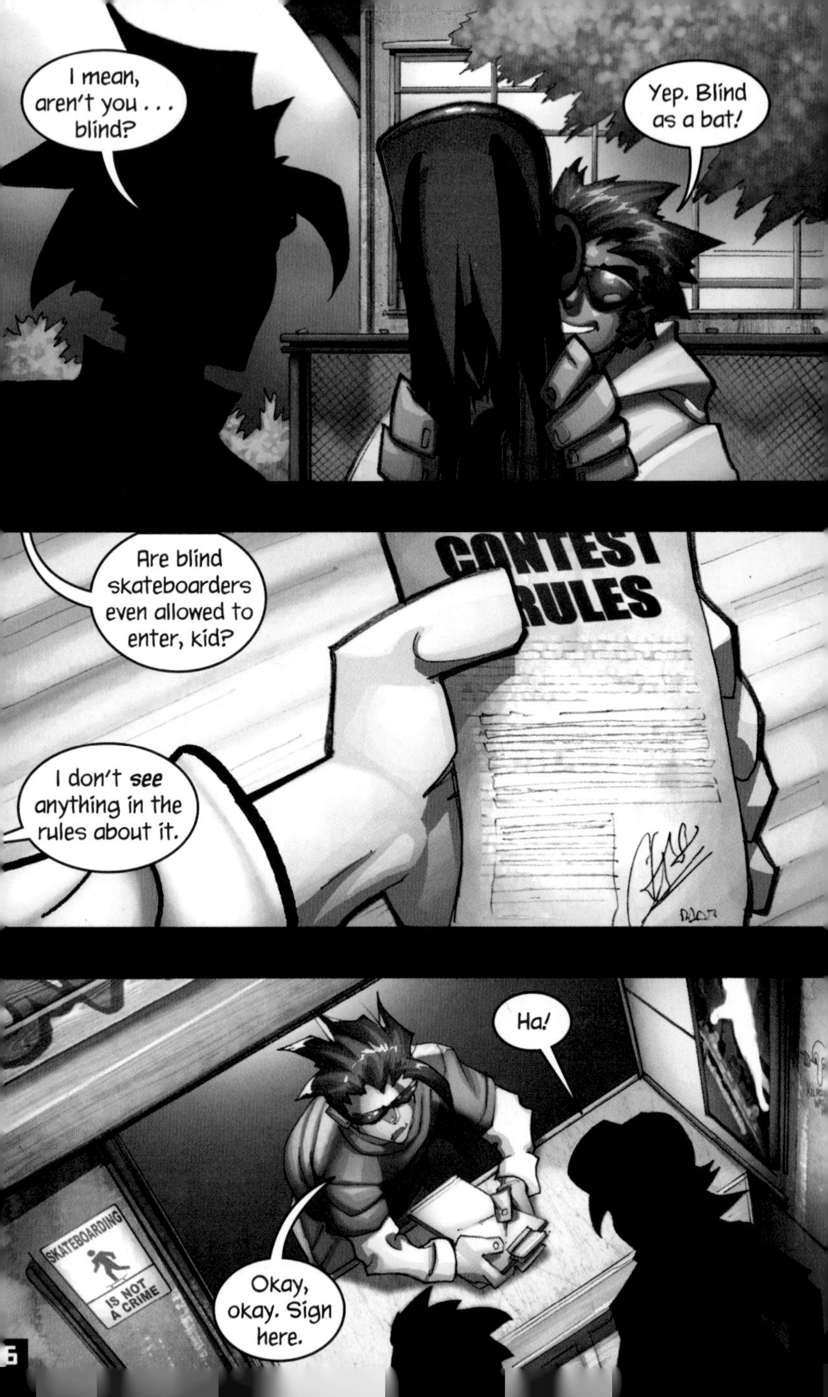

I mean, aren't you . . . blind?
Yep. Blind as a bat!
Are blind skateboarders even allowed to enter, kid?
CONTEST RULES
I don't *see* anything in the rules about it.
Ha!
SKATEBOARDING IS NOT A CRIME
Okay, okay. Sign here.

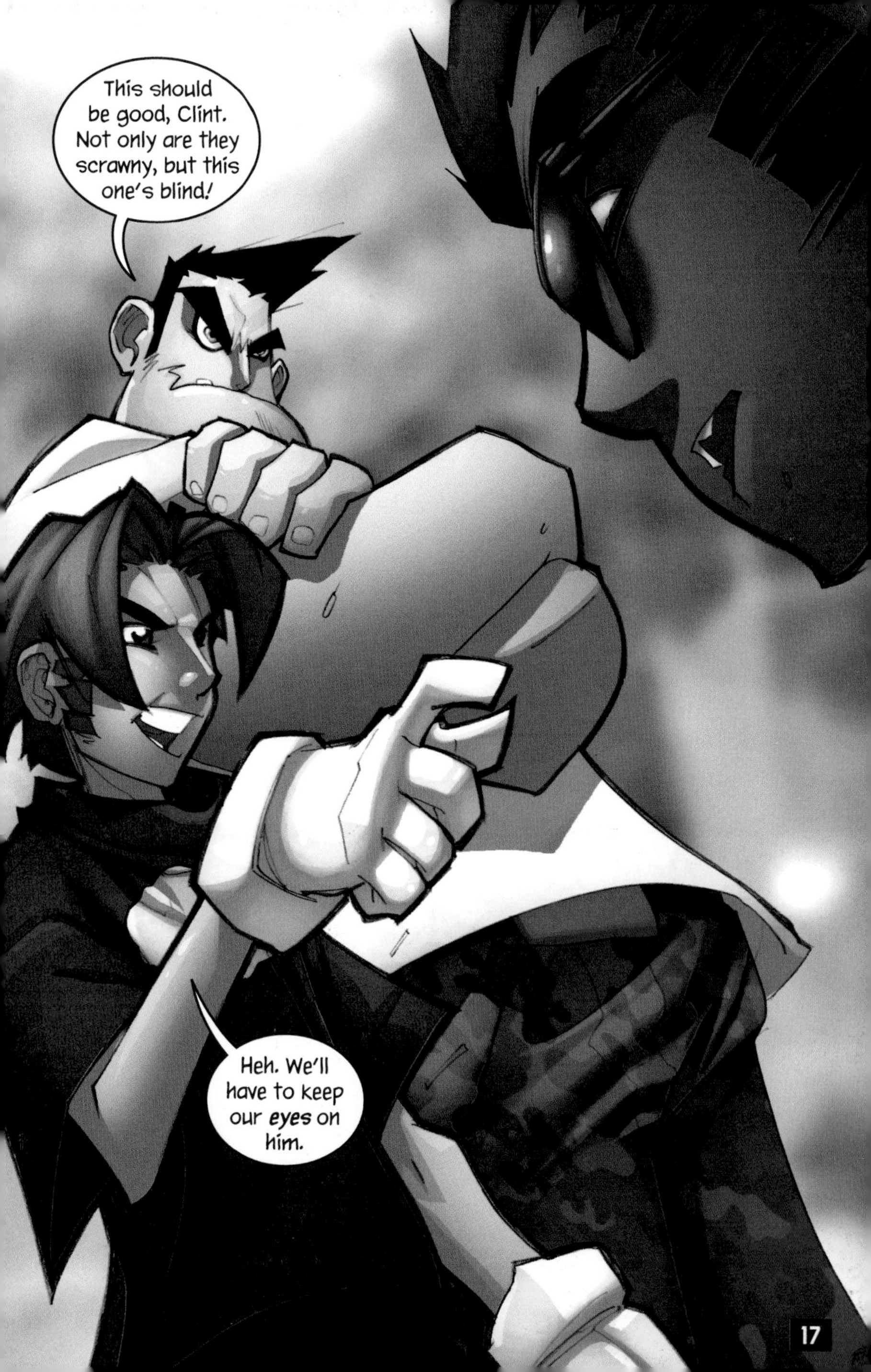
This should be good, Clint. Not only are they scrawny, but this one's blind!
Heh. We'll have to keep our *eyes* on him.

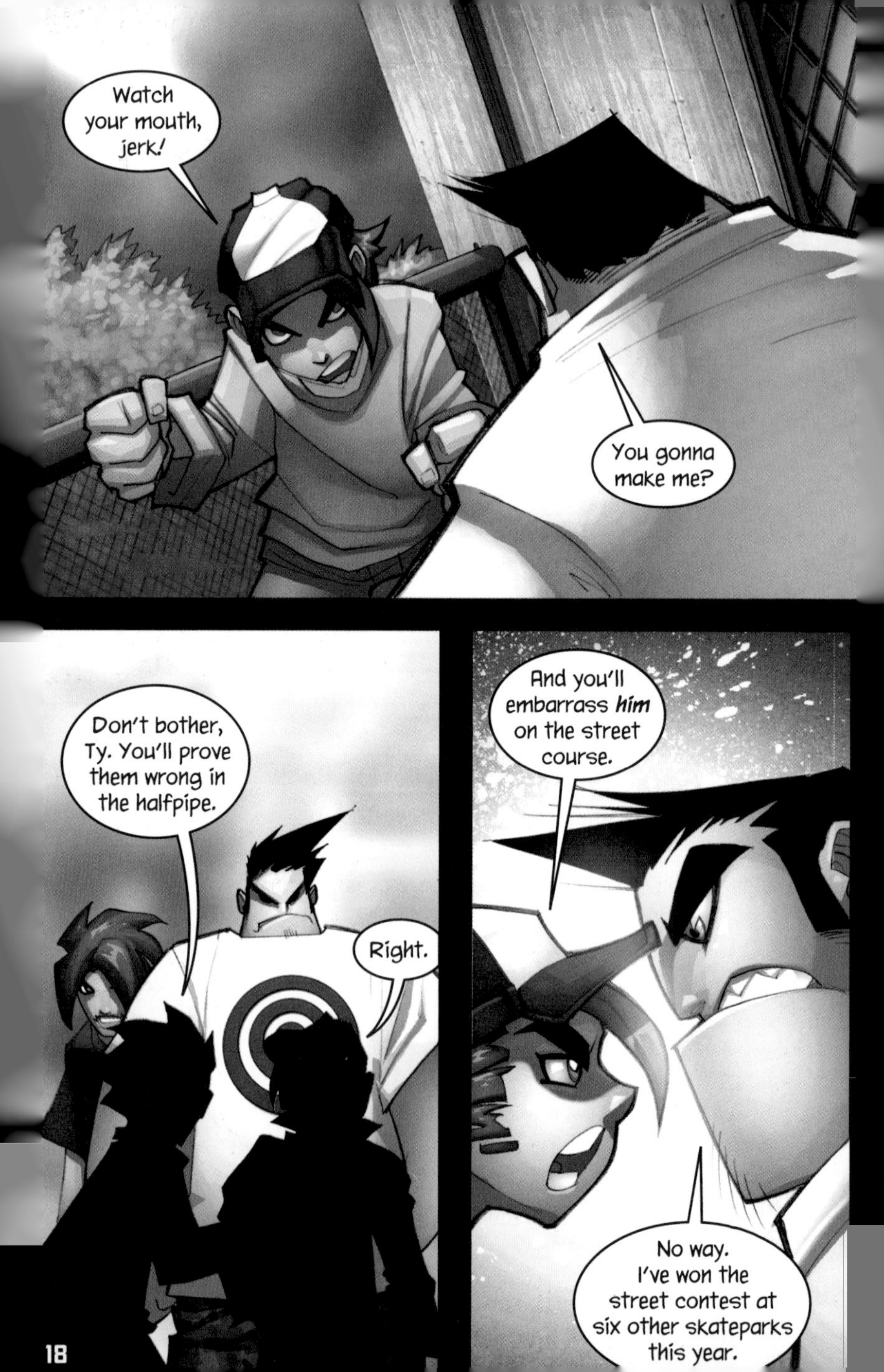
Watch your mouth, jerk!
You gonna make me?
Don't bother, Ty. You'll prove them wrong in the halfpipe.
Right.
And you'll embarrass *him* on the street course.
No way. I've won the street contest at six other skateparks this year.

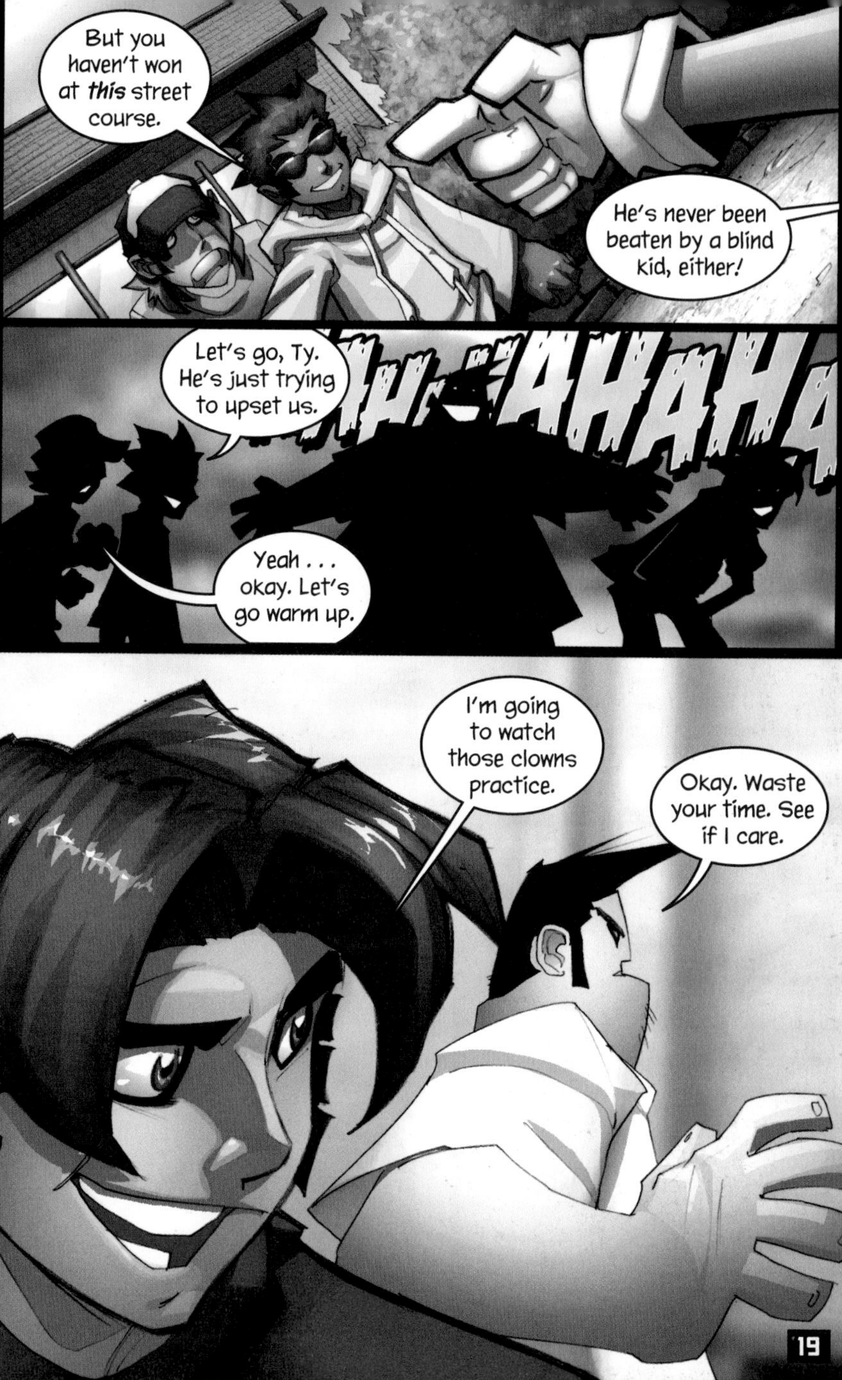
But you haven't won at *this* street course.
He's never been beaten by a blind kid, either!
Let's go, Ty. He's just trying to upset us.
AHAHA
Yeah . . . okay. Let's go warm up.
I'm going to watch those clowns practice.
Okay. Waste your time. See if I care.

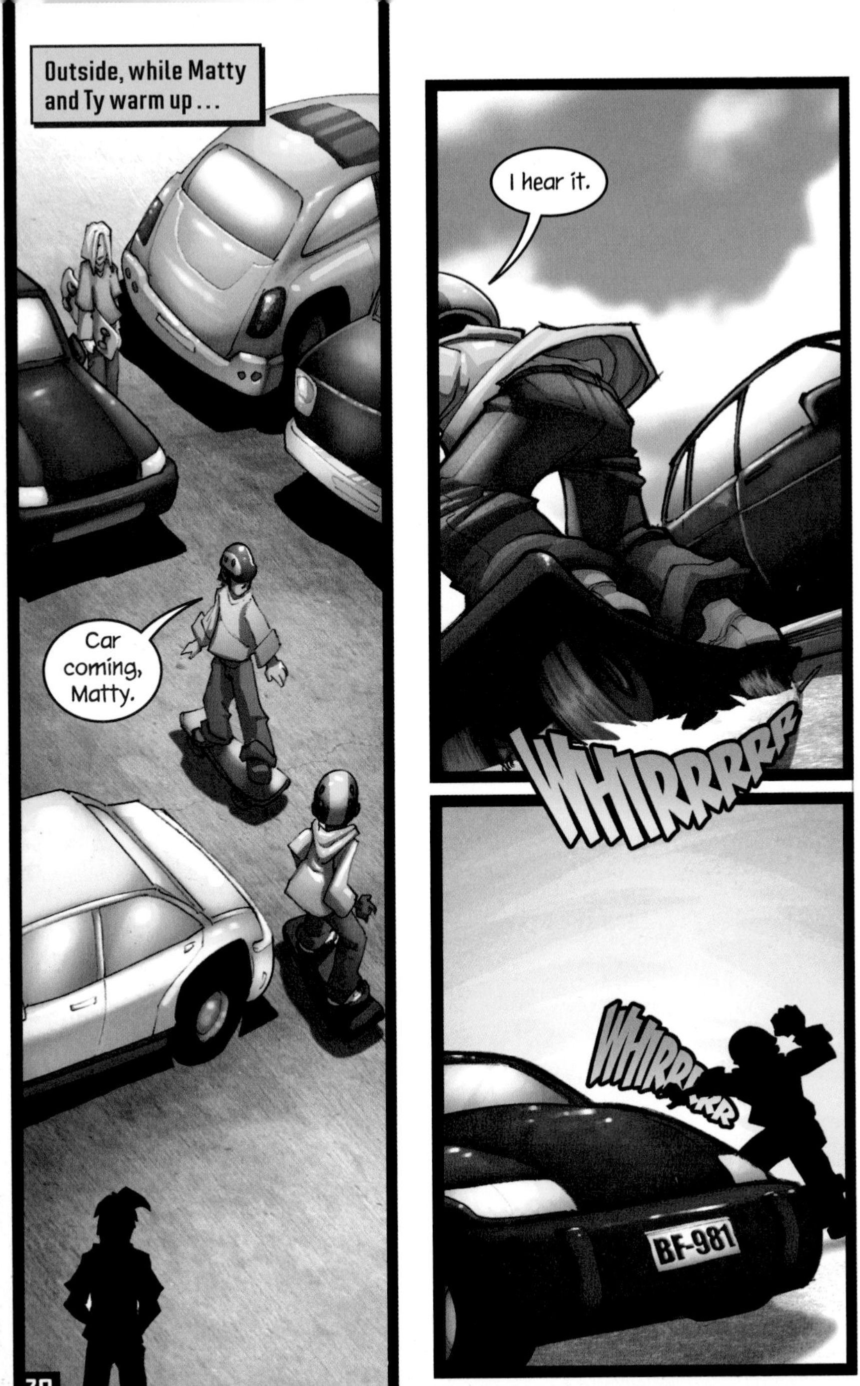
Outside, while Matty and Ty warm up . . .
Car coming, Matty.
I hear it.
WHIRRRRR
WHIRRRRR

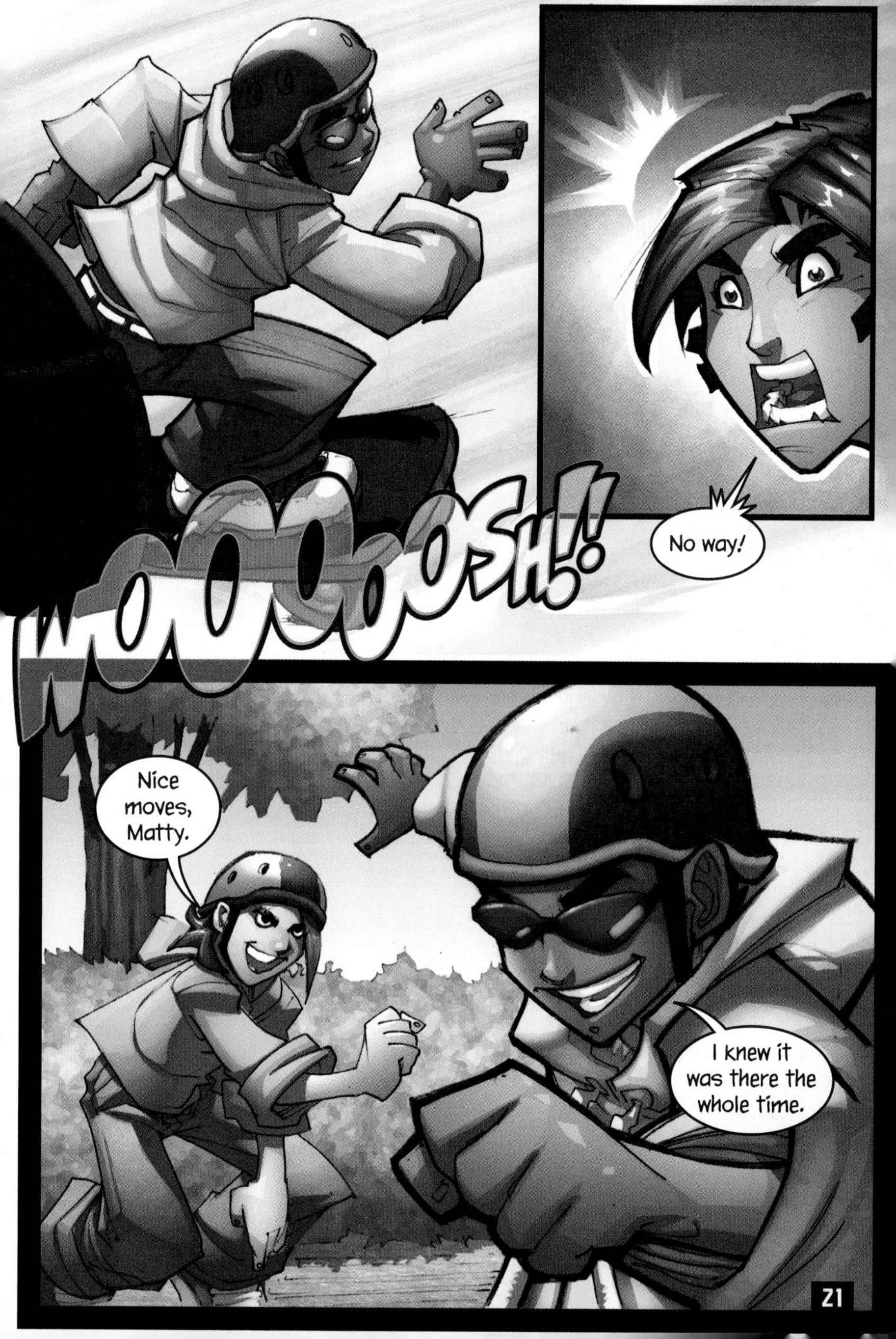
WOOOOOOSH!!
No way!
Nice moves, Matty.
I knew it was there the whole time.

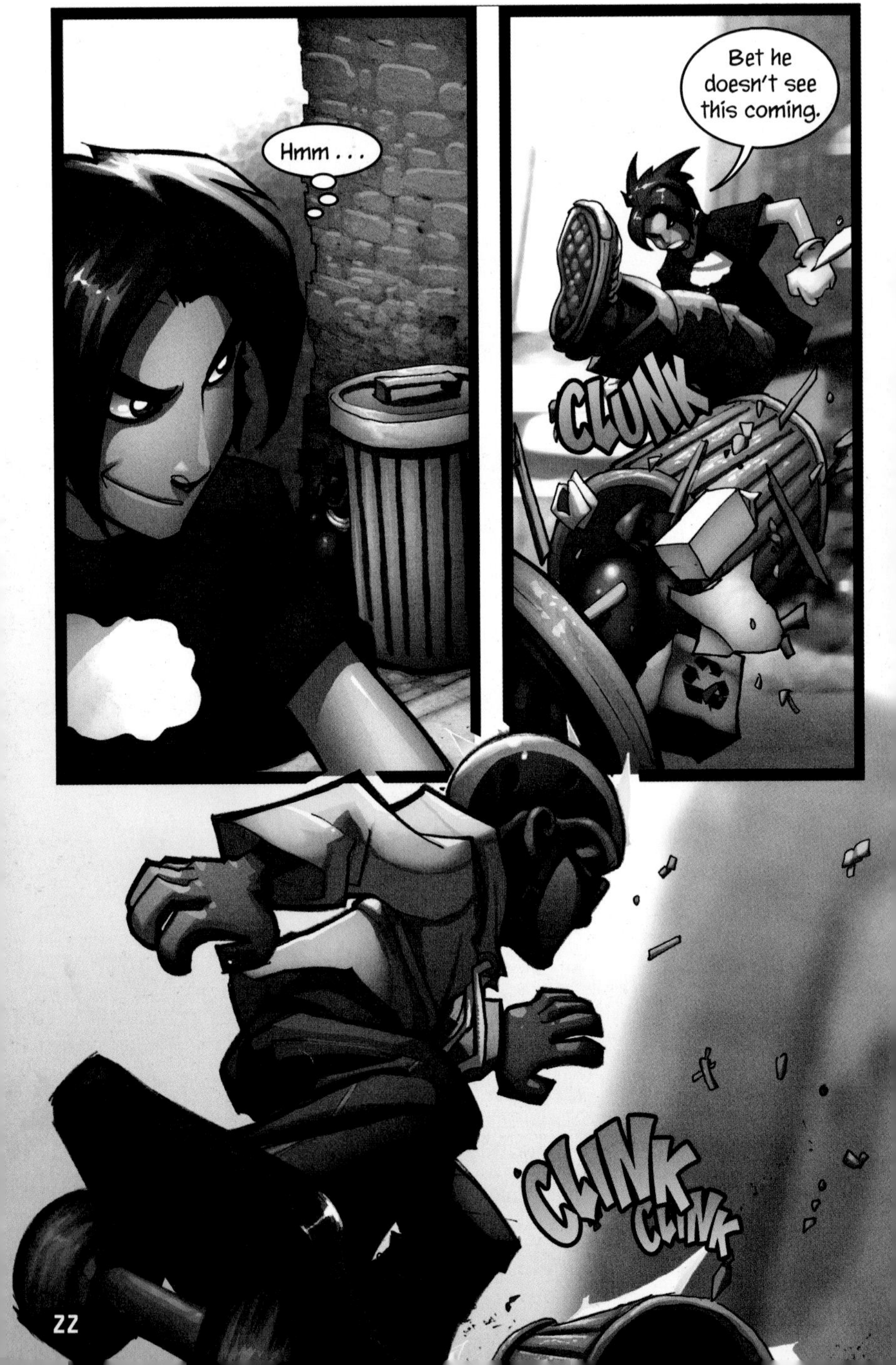

Hmm . . .
Bet he doesn't see this coming.
CLUNK
CLINK
CLINK

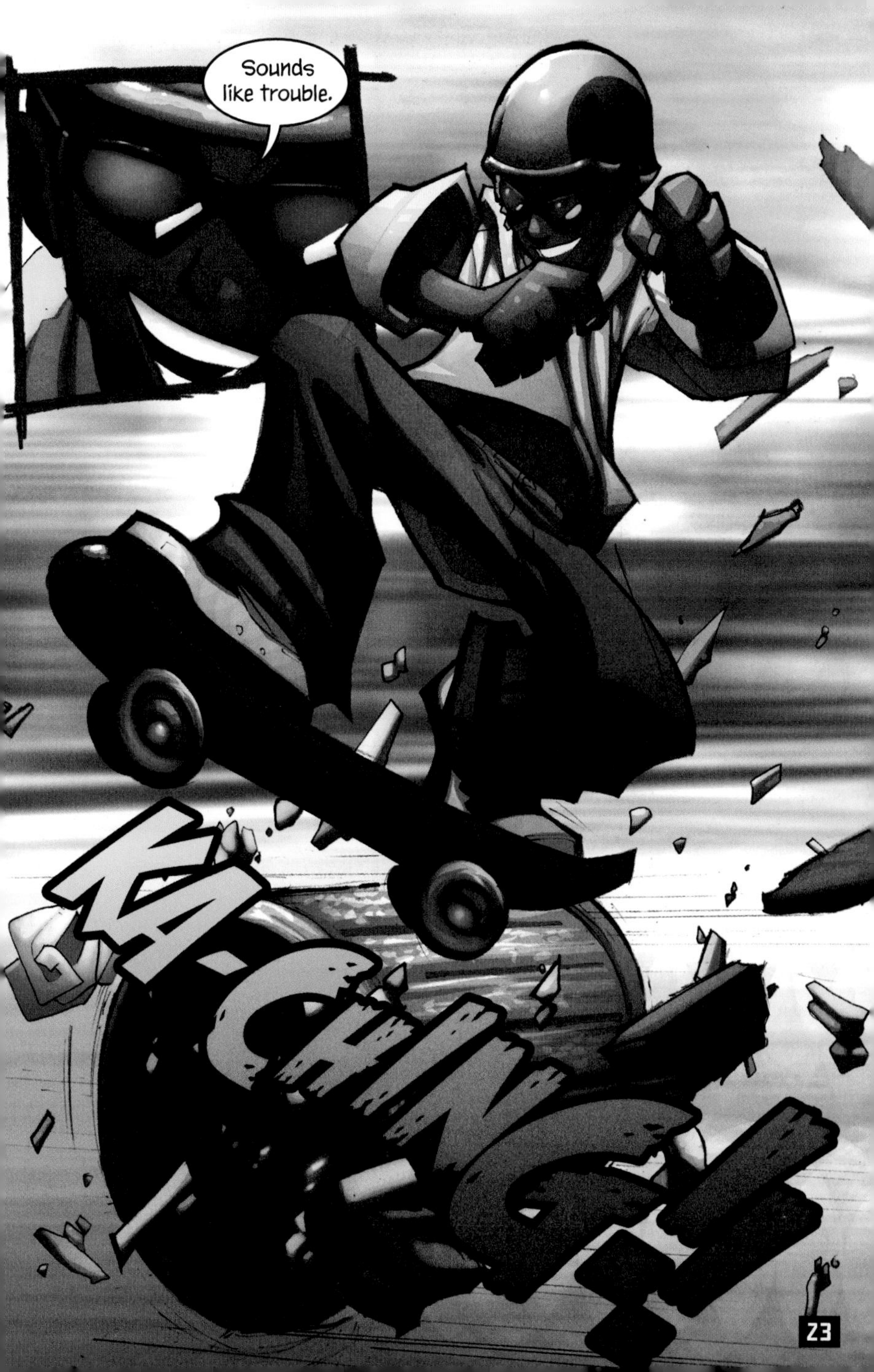
Sounds like trouble.
KA-CHING!

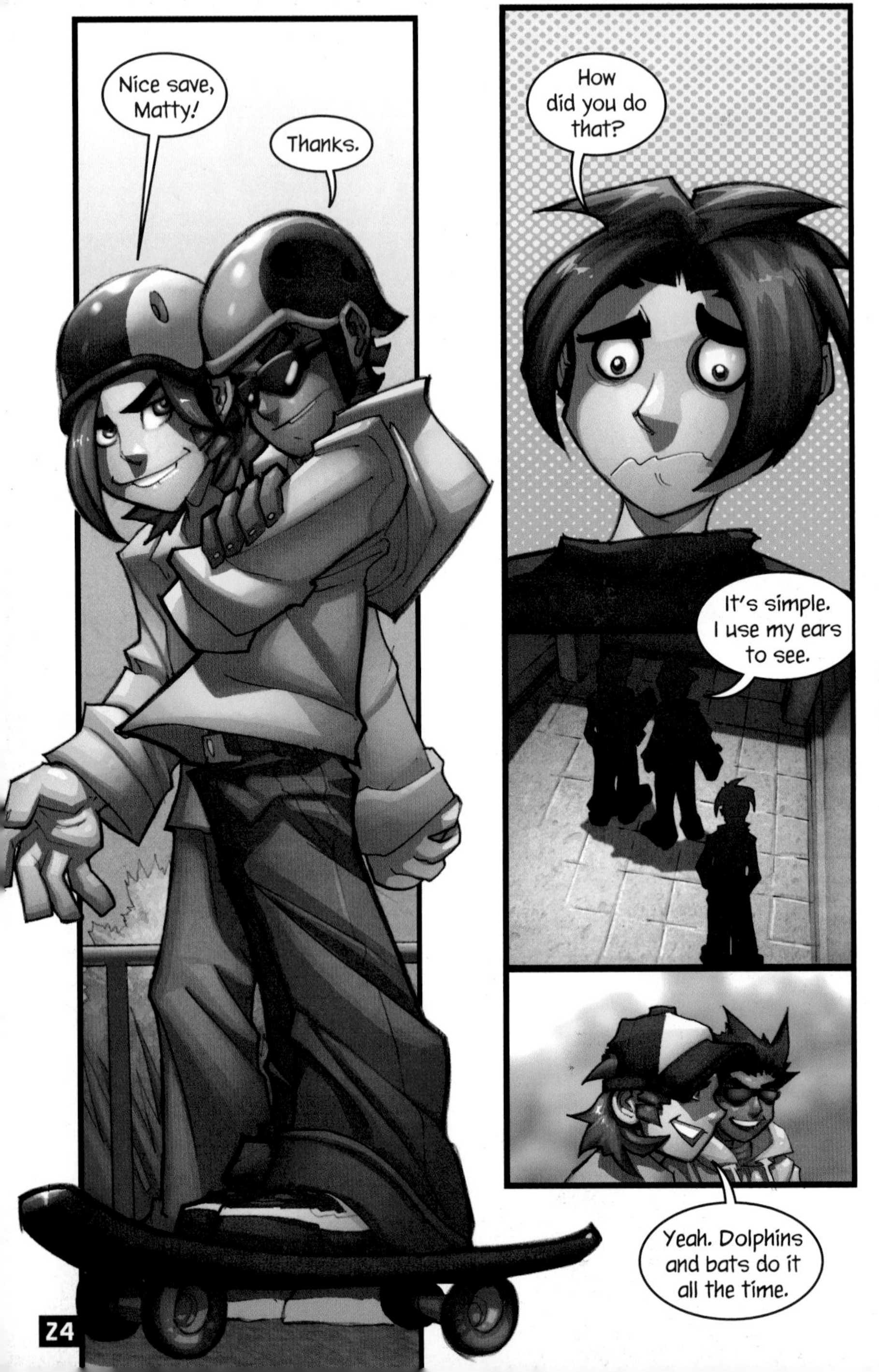
Nice save, Matty!
Thanks.
How did you do that?
It's simple. I use my ears to see.
Yeah. Dolphins and bats do it all the time.

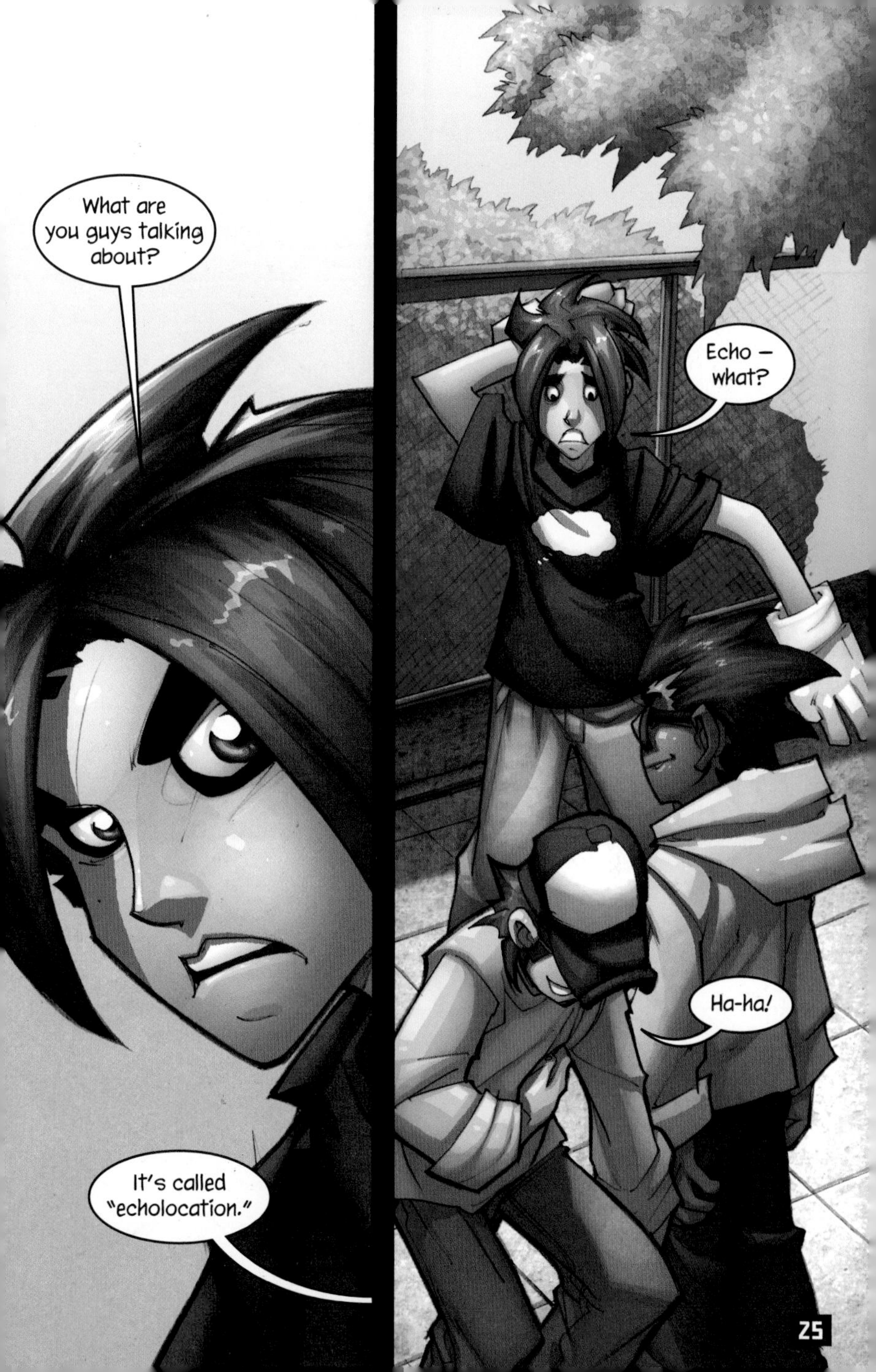
What are you guys talking about?
It's called "echolocation."
Echo – what?
Ha-ha!

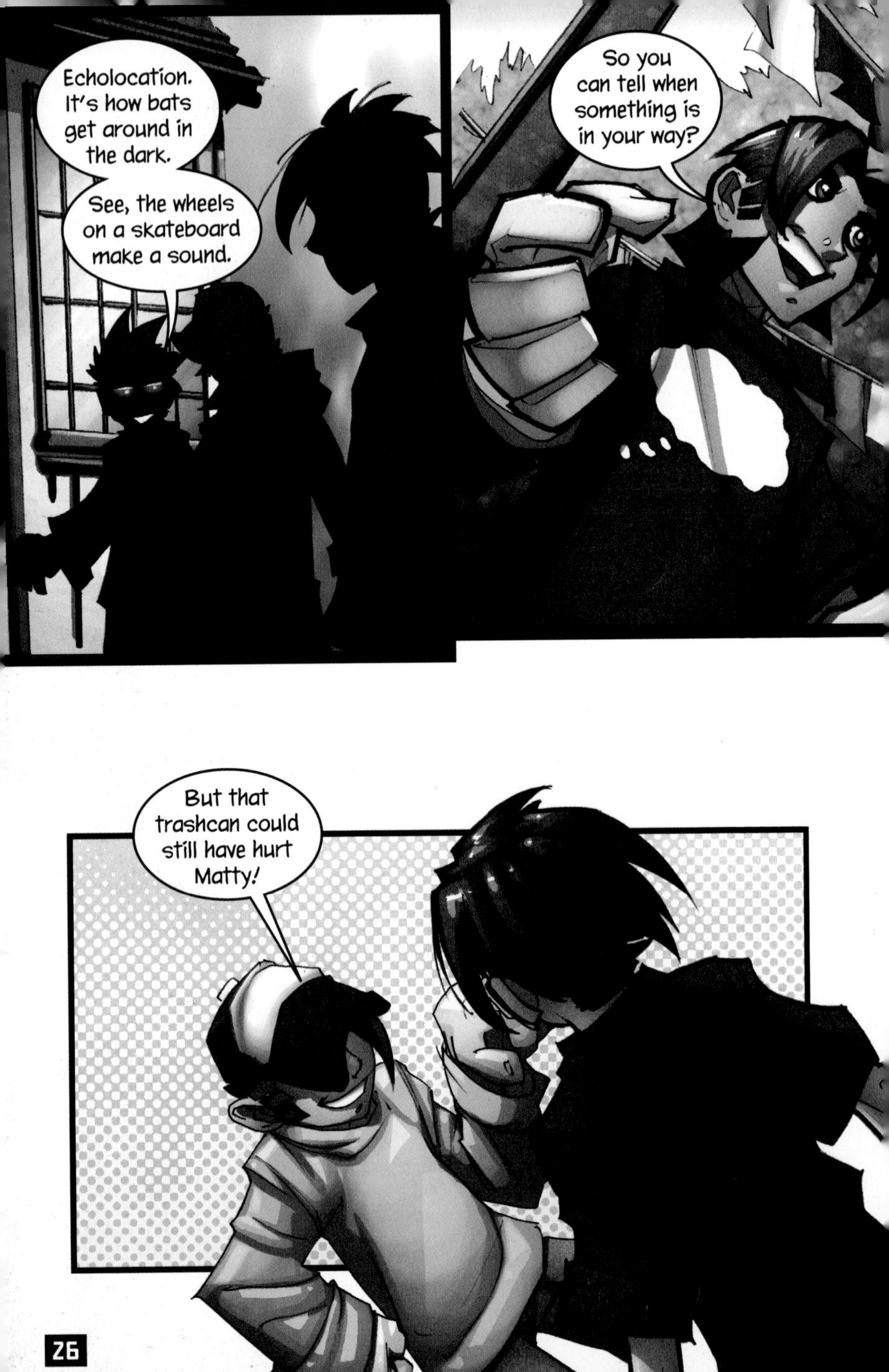
Echolocation. It's how bats get around in the dark.
See, the wheels on a skateboard make a sound.
So you can tell when something is in your way?
But that trashcan could still have hurt Matty!

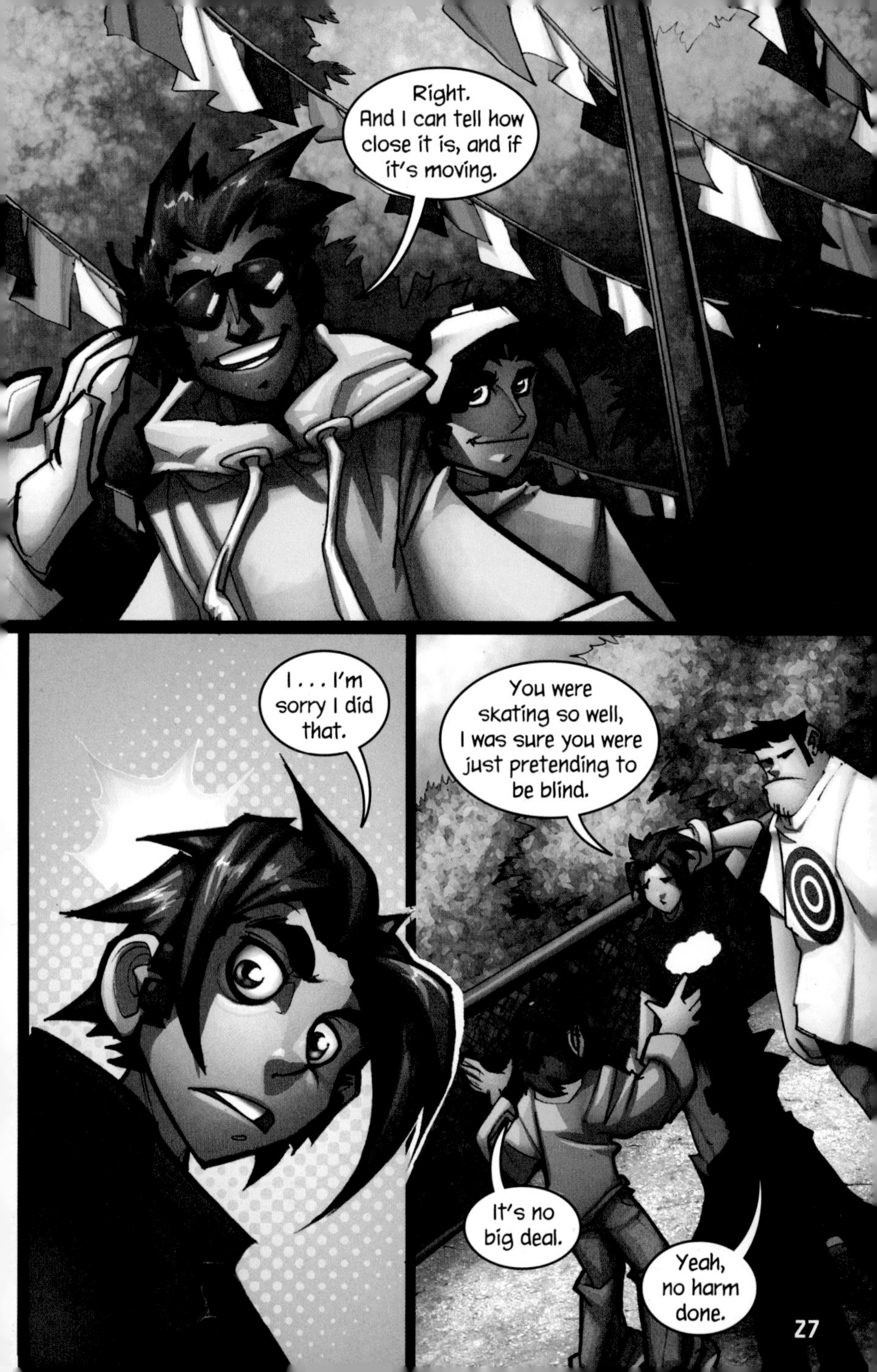
Right. And I can tell how close it is, and if it's moving.
I . . . I'm sorry I did that.
You were skating so well, I was sure you were just pretending to be blind.
It's no big deal.
Yeah, no harm done.

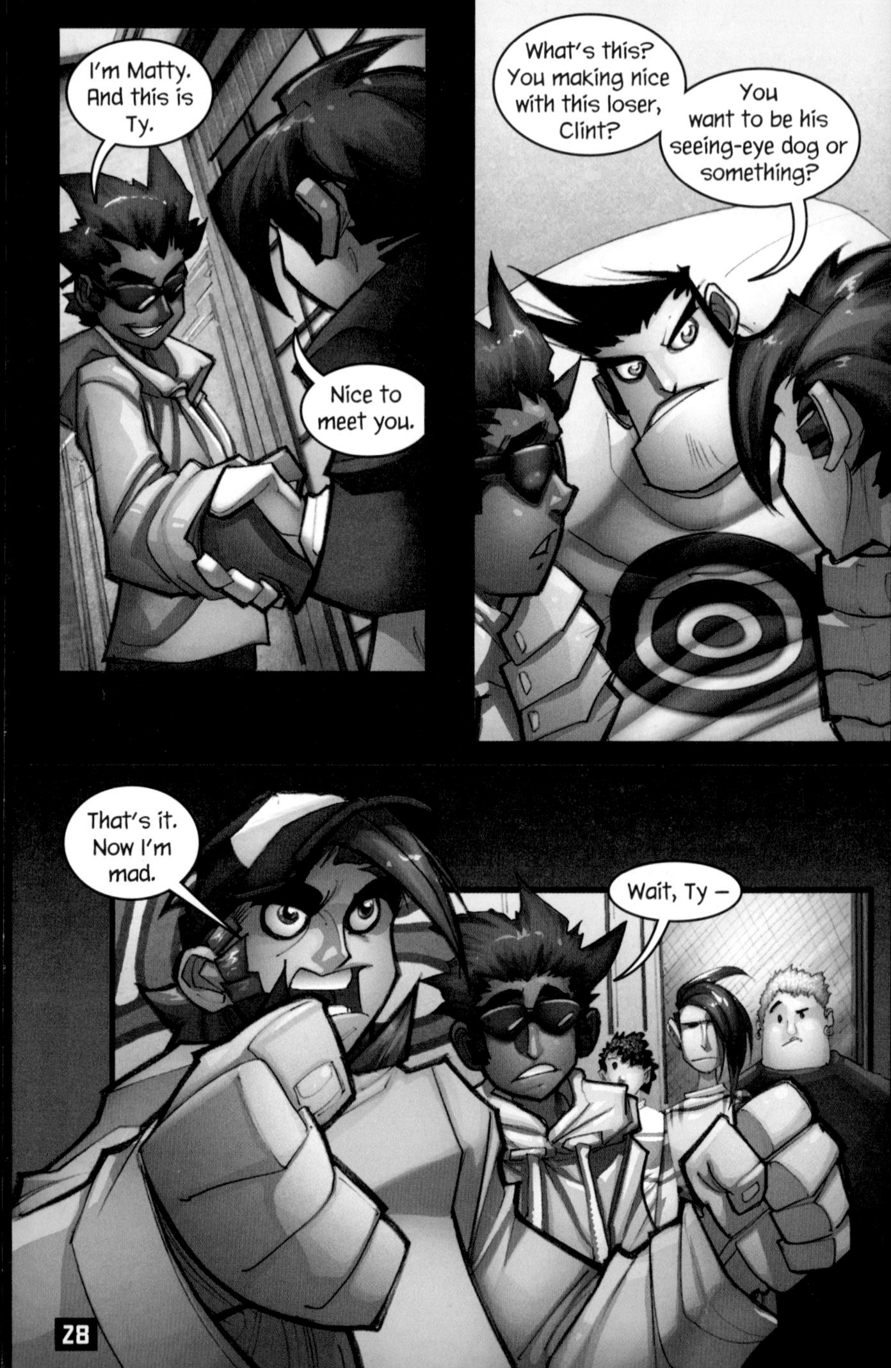
I'm Matty. And this is Ty.
Nice to meet you.
What's this? You making nice with this loser, Clint?
You want to be his seeing-eye dog or something?
That's it. Now I'm mad.
Wait, Ty —

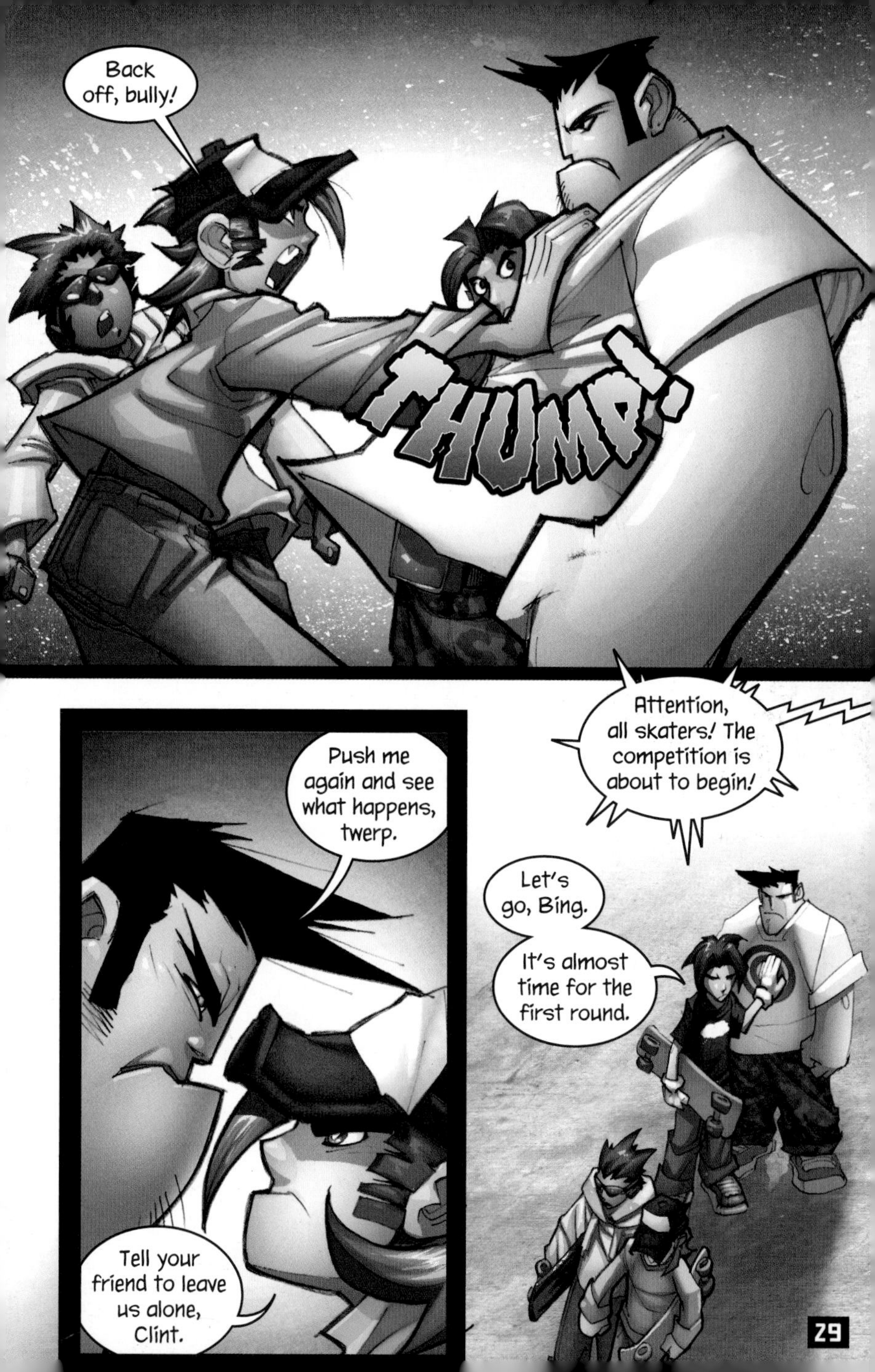
Back off, bully!
THUMP!
Push me again and see what happens, twerp.
Tell your friend to leave us alone, Clint.
Attention, all skaters! The competition is about to begin!
Let's go, Bing.
It's almost time for the first round.

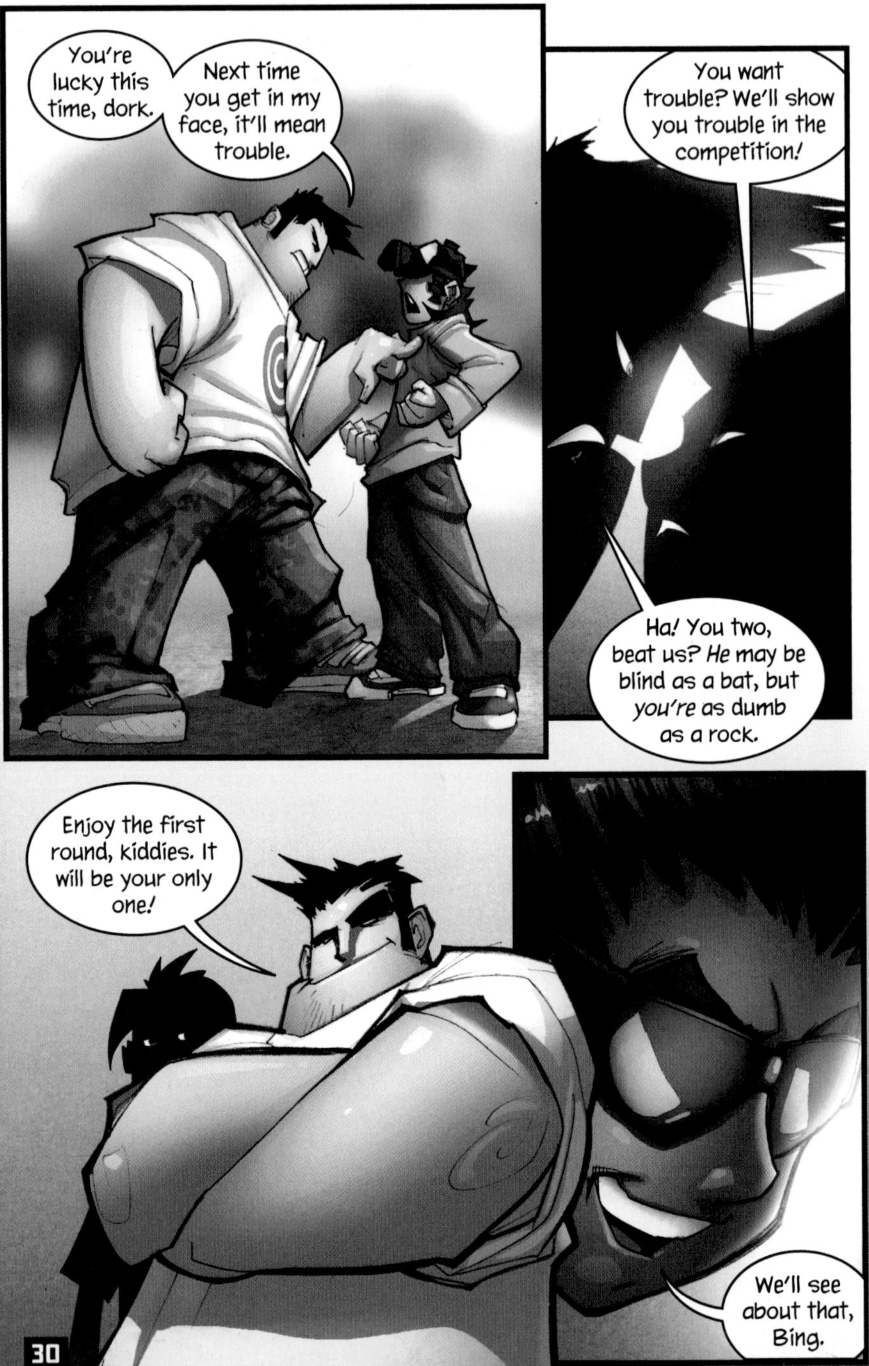
You're lucky this time, dork.
Next time you get in my face, it'll mean trouble.
You want trouble? We'll show you trouble in the competition!
Ha! You two, beat us? *He* may be blind as a bat, but *you're* as dumb as a rock.
Enjoy the first round, kiddies. It will be your only one!
We'll see about that, Bing.

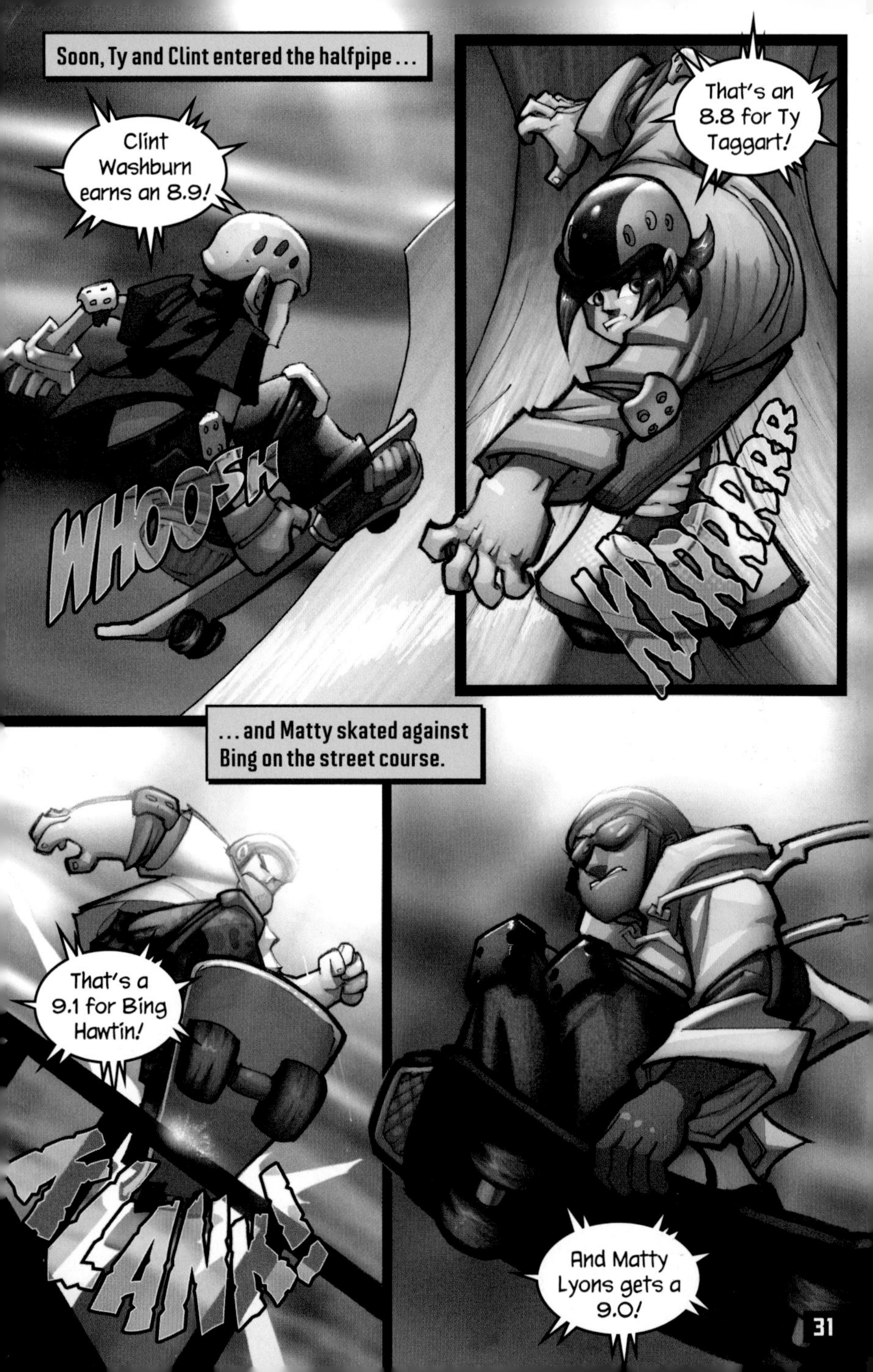
Soon, Ty and Clint entered the halfpipe . . .
Clint Washburn earns an 8.9!
WHOOSH
That's an 8.8 for Ty Taggart!
. . . and Matty skated against Bing on the street course.
That's a 9.1 for Bing Hawtin!
And Matty Lyons gets a 9.0!

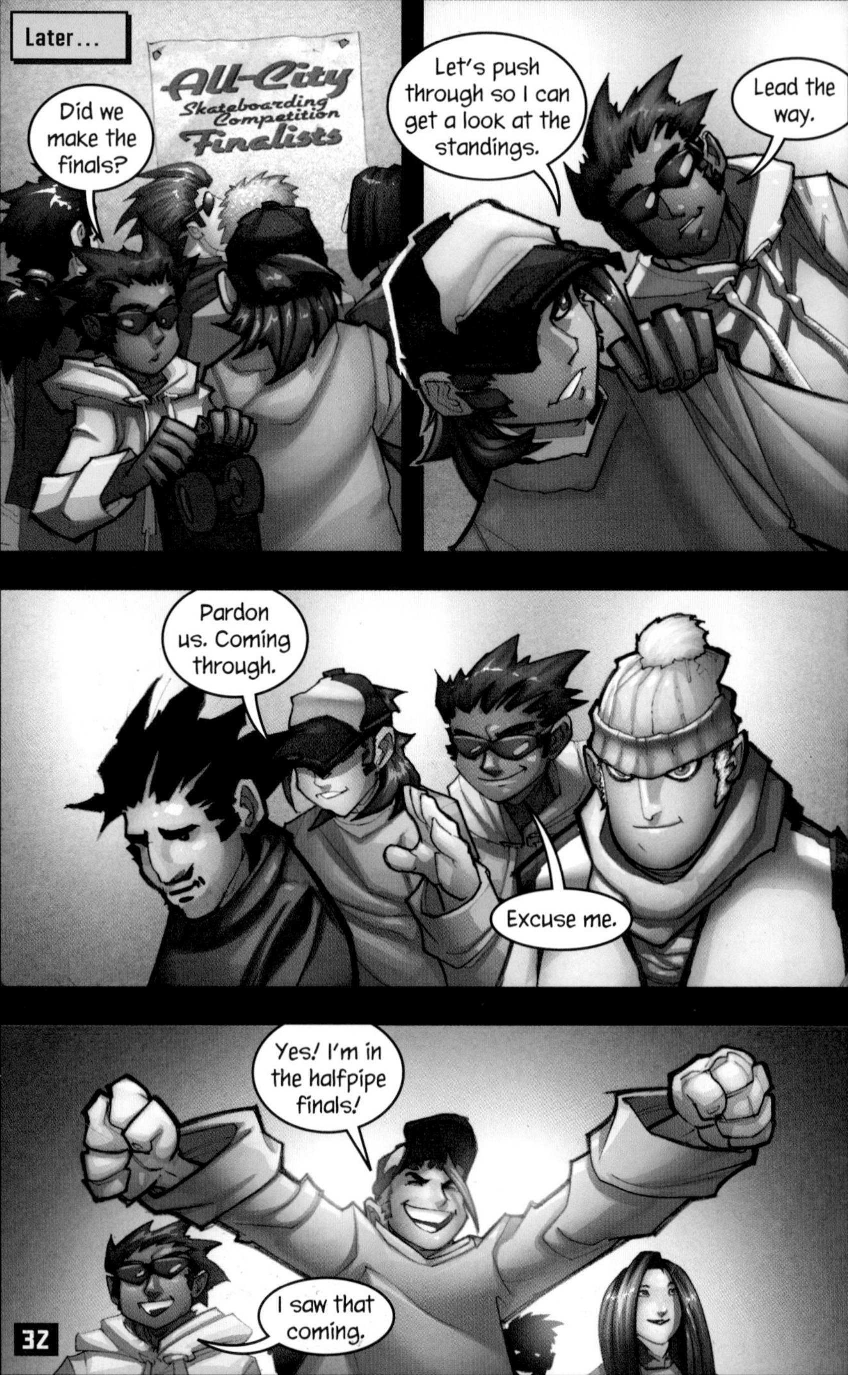

Later...
All-City Skateboarding Competition Finalists
Did we make the finals?
Let's push through so I can get a look at the standings.
Lead the way.
Pardon us. Coming through.
Excuse me.
Yes! I'm in the halfpipe finals!
I saw that coming.

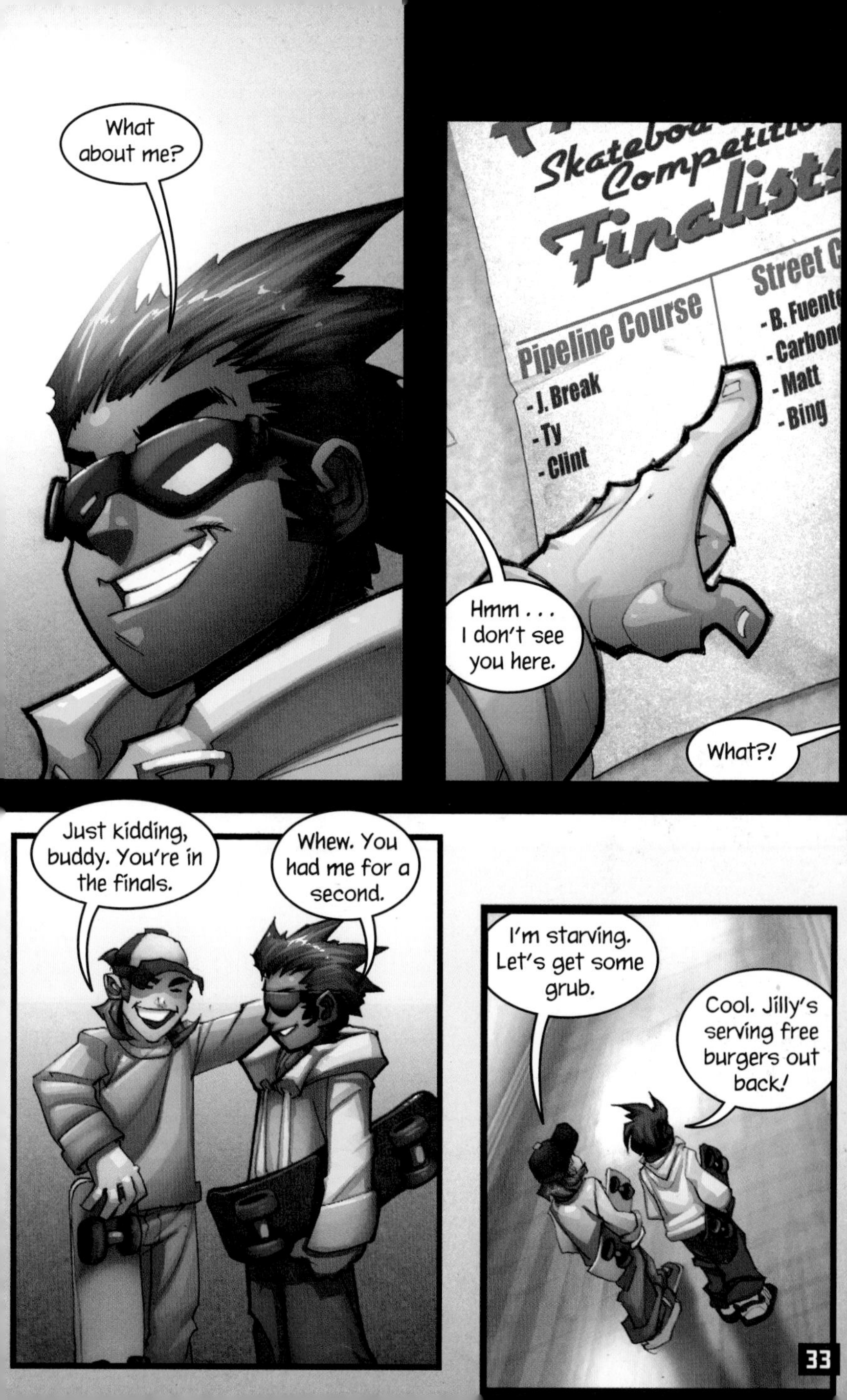
What about me?
Skateboard Competition Finalists
Pipeline Course
- J. Break
- Ty
- Clint
Street C
- B. Fuente
- Carbon
- Matt
- Bing
Hmm . . . I don't see you here.
What?!
Just kidding, buddy. You're in the finals.
Whew. You had me for a second.
I'm starving. Let's get some grub.
Cool. Jilly's serving free burgers out back!

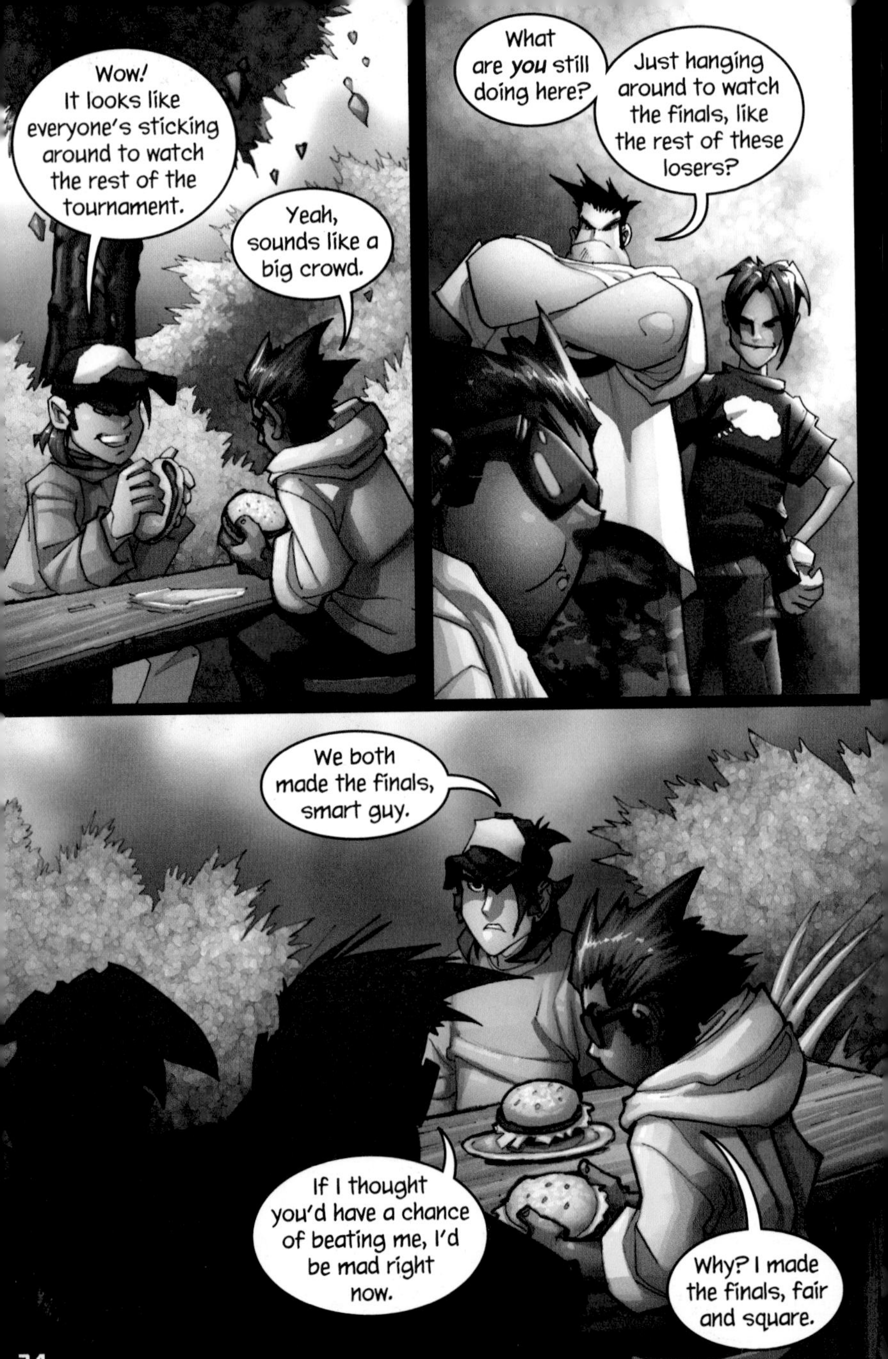
Wow! It looks like everyone's sticking around to watch the rest of the tournament.
Yeah, sounds like a big crowd.
What are *you* still doing here?
Just hanging around to watch the finals, like the rest of these losers?
We both made the finals, smart guy.
If I thought you'd have a chance of beating me, I'd be mad right now.
Why? I made the finals, fair and square.

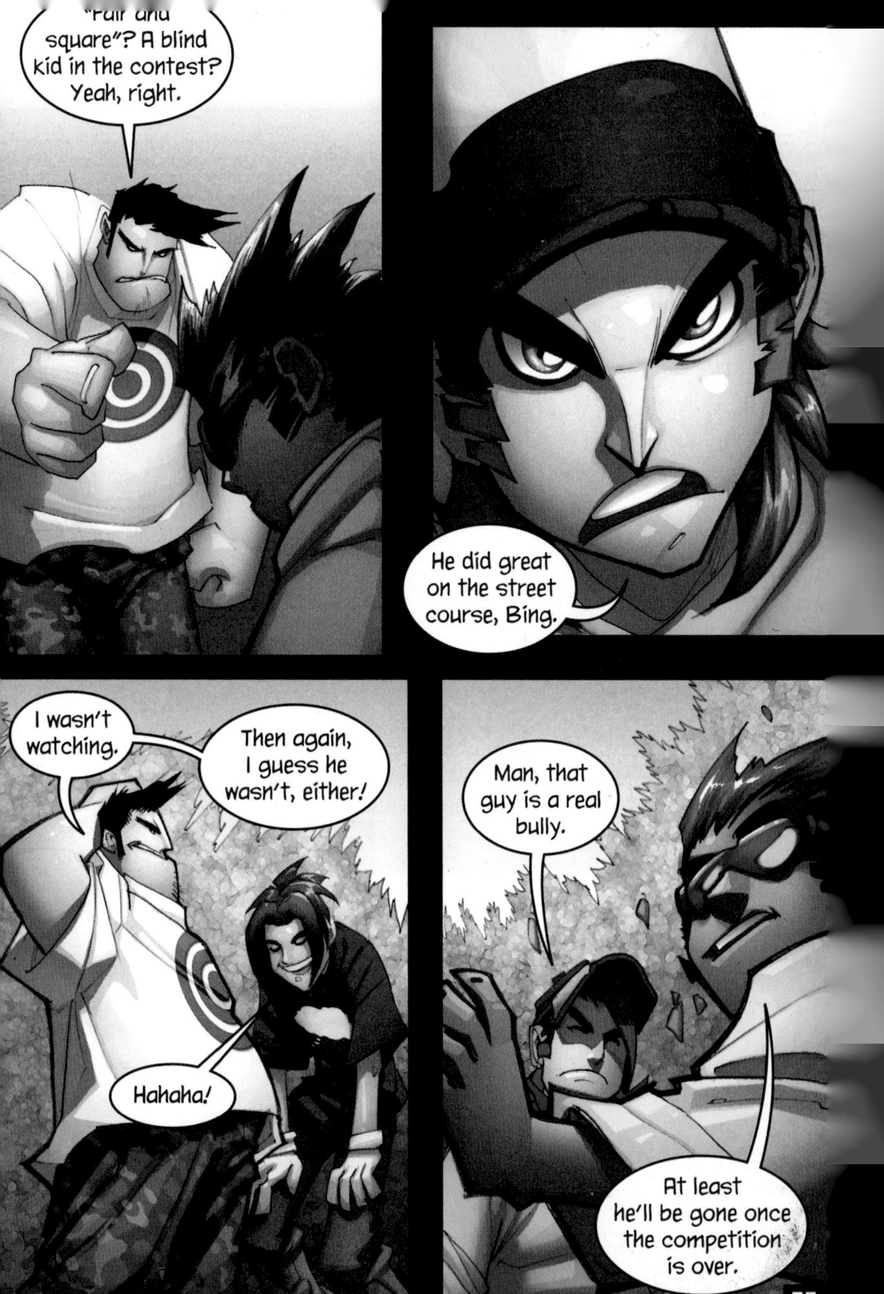
"Fair and square"? A blind kid in the contest? Yeah, right.
He did great on the street course, Bing.
I wasn't watching.
Then again, I guess he wasn't, either!
Hahaha!
Man, that guy is a real bully.
At least he'll be gone once the competition is over.

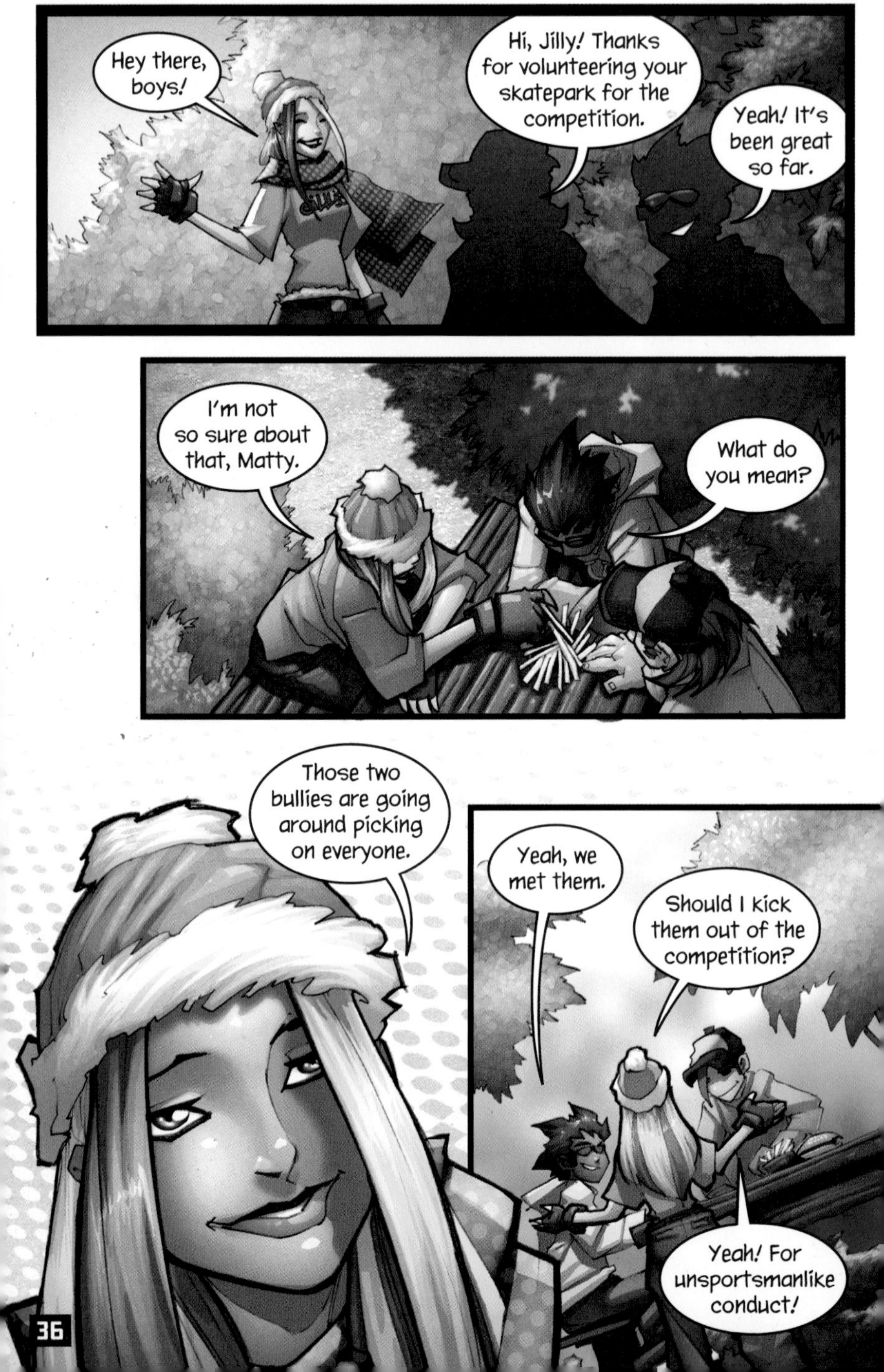
Hey there, boys!
Hi, Jilly! Thanks for volunteering your skatepark for the competition.
Yeah! It's been great so far.
I'm not so sure about that, Matty.
What do you mean?
Those two bullies are going around picking on everyone.
Yeah, we met them.
Should I kick them out of the competition?
Yeah! For unsportsmanlike conduct!

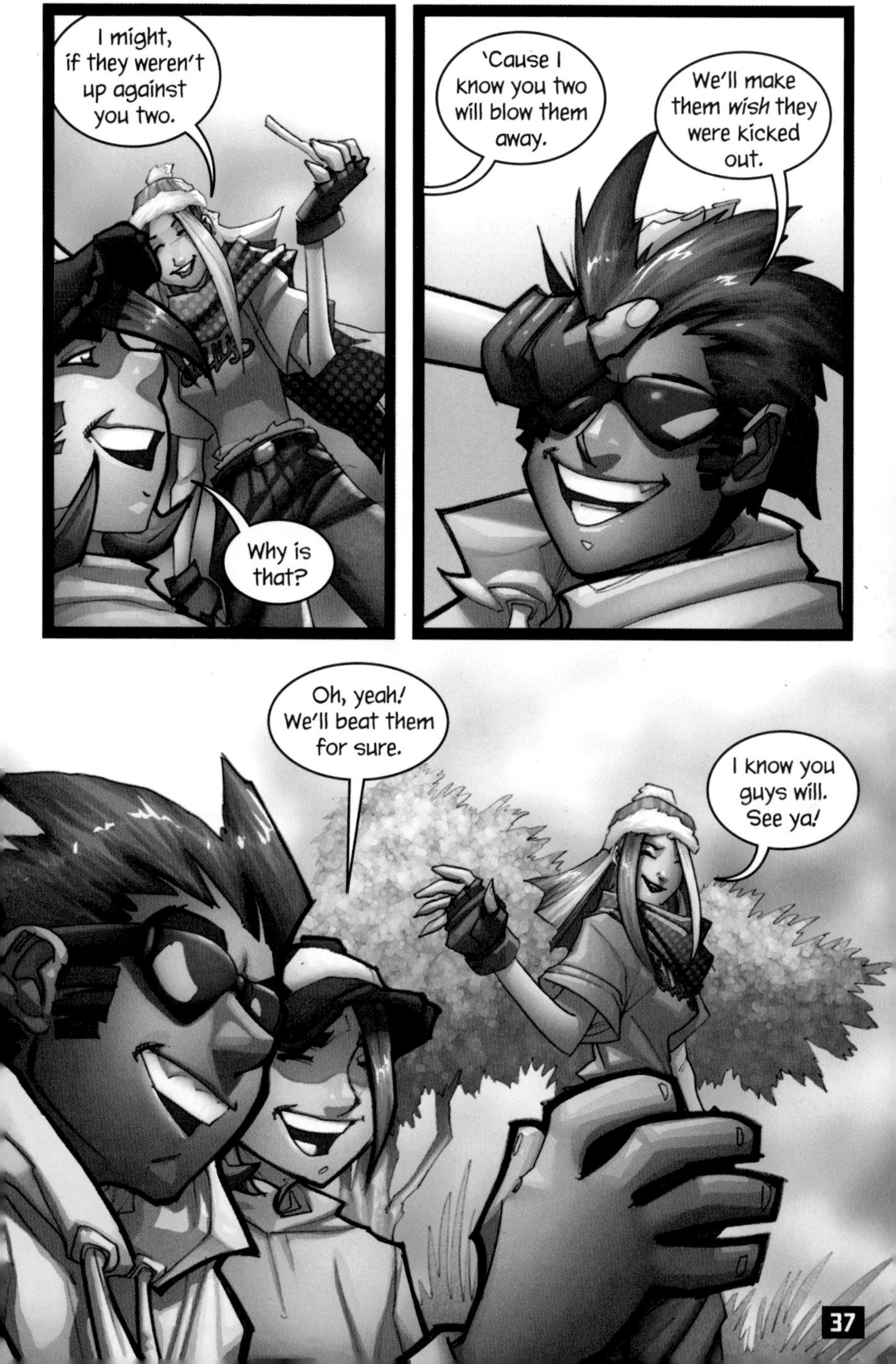
I might, if they weren't up against you two.
Why is that?
'Cause I know you two will blow them away.
We'll make them *wish* they were kicked out.
Oh, yeah! We'll beat them for sure.
I know you guys will. See ya!

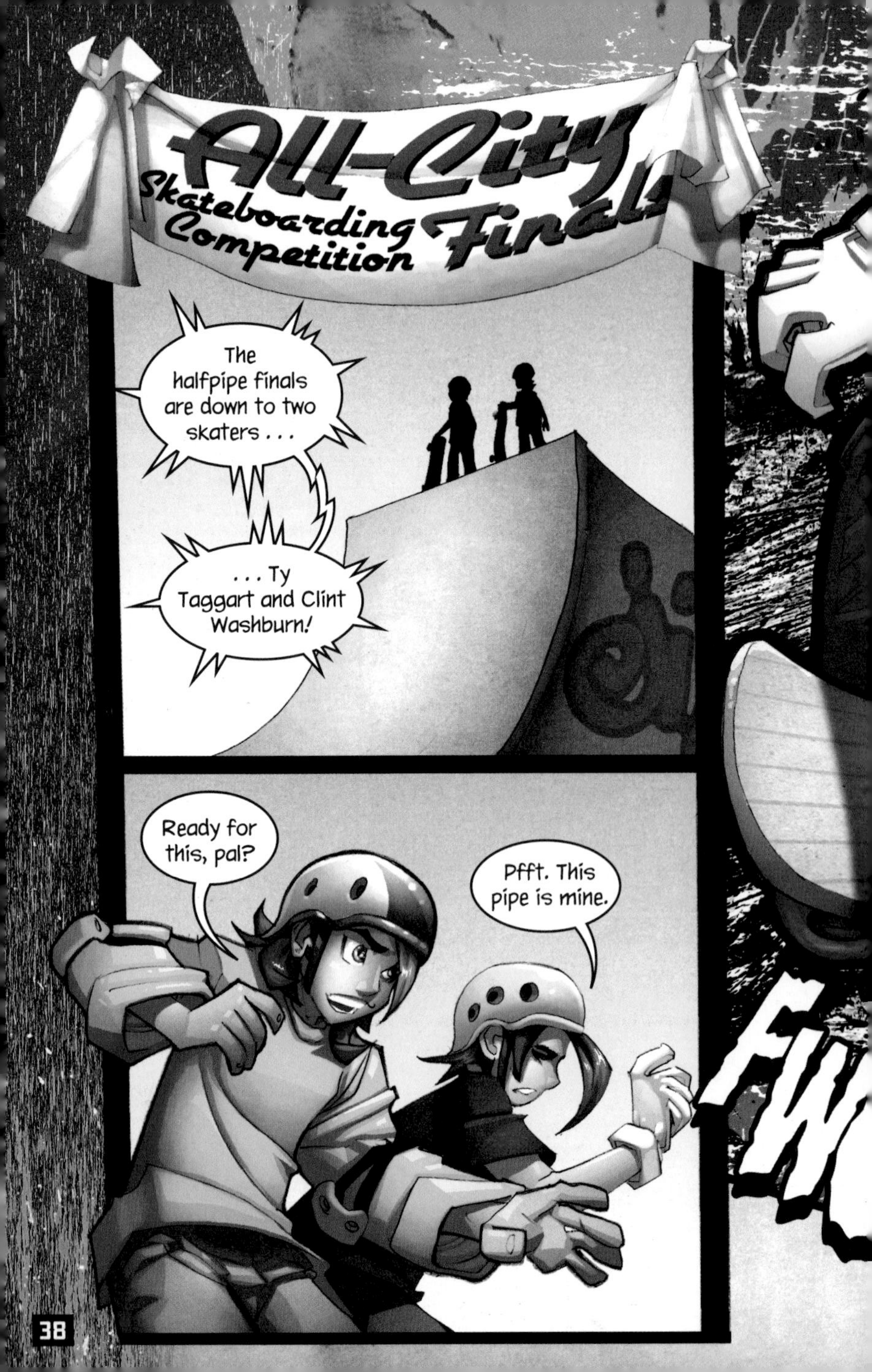
All-City Skateboarding Competition Finals
The halfpipe finals are down to two skaters . . .
. . . Ty Taggart and Clint Washburn!
Ready for this, pal?
Pfft. This pipe is mine.

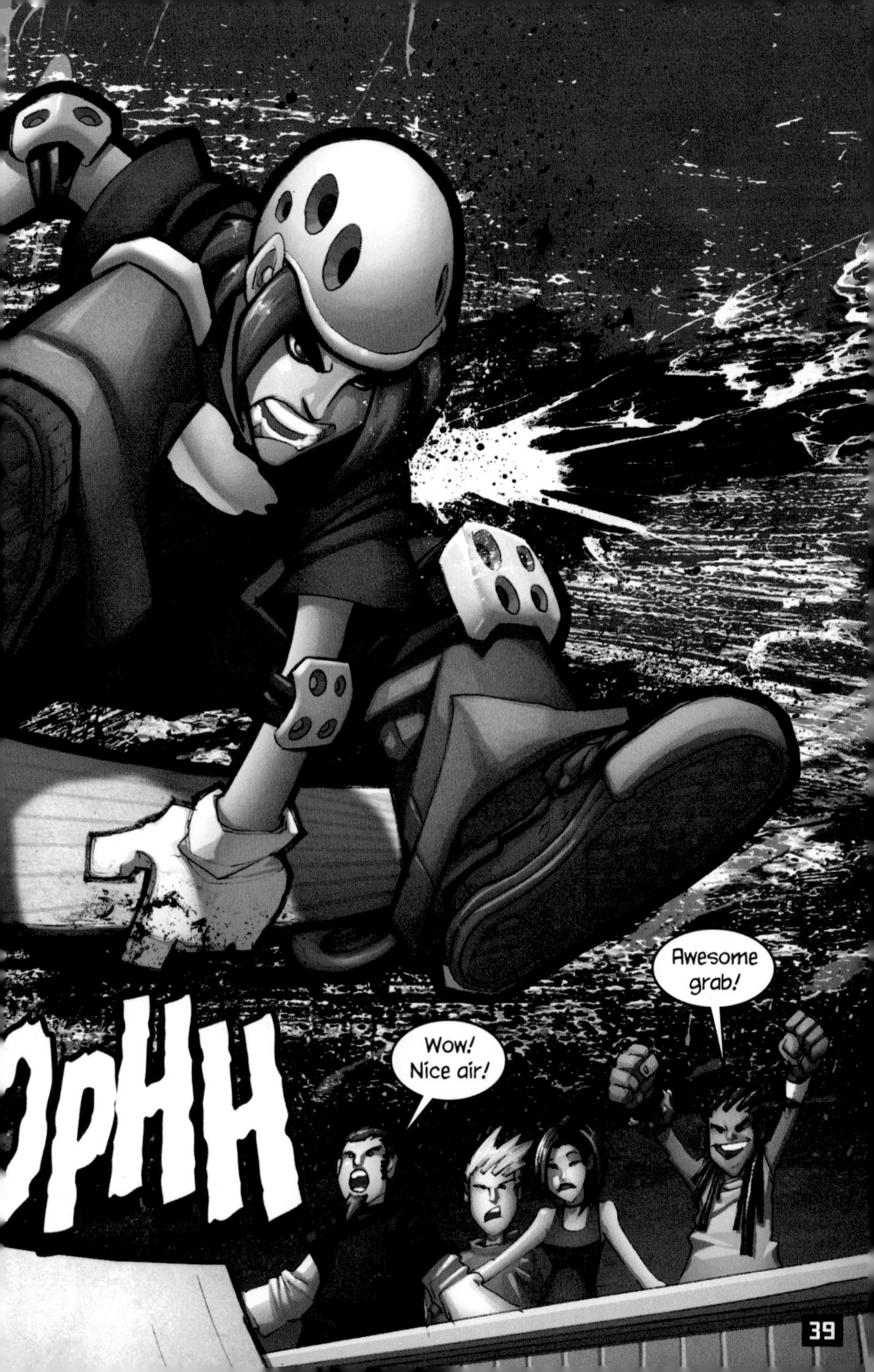

OPHH
Wow! Nice air!
Awesome grab!

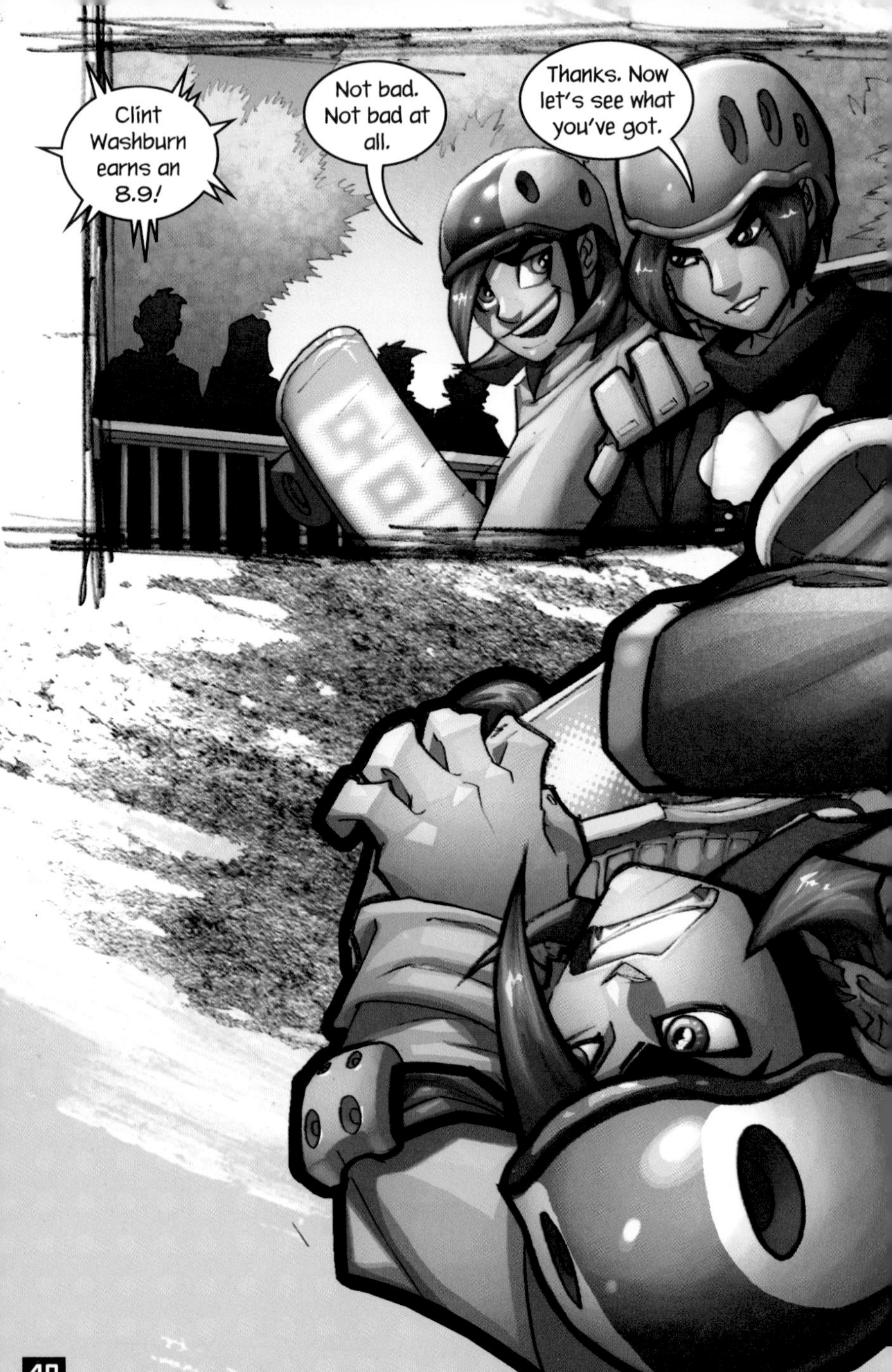
Clint Washburn earns an 8.9!
Not bad. Not bad at all.
Thanks. Now let's see what you've got.

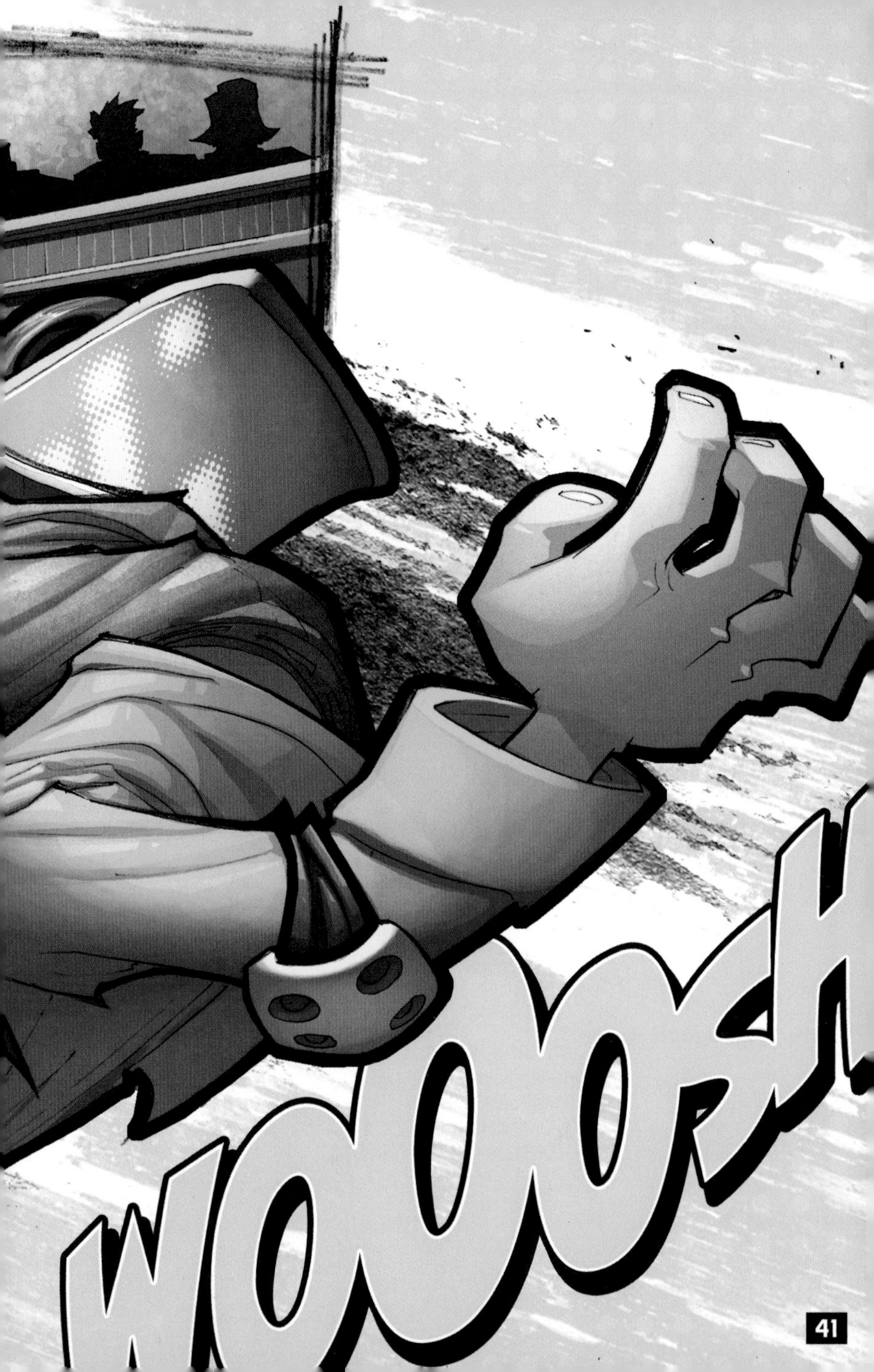
WOOOSH!

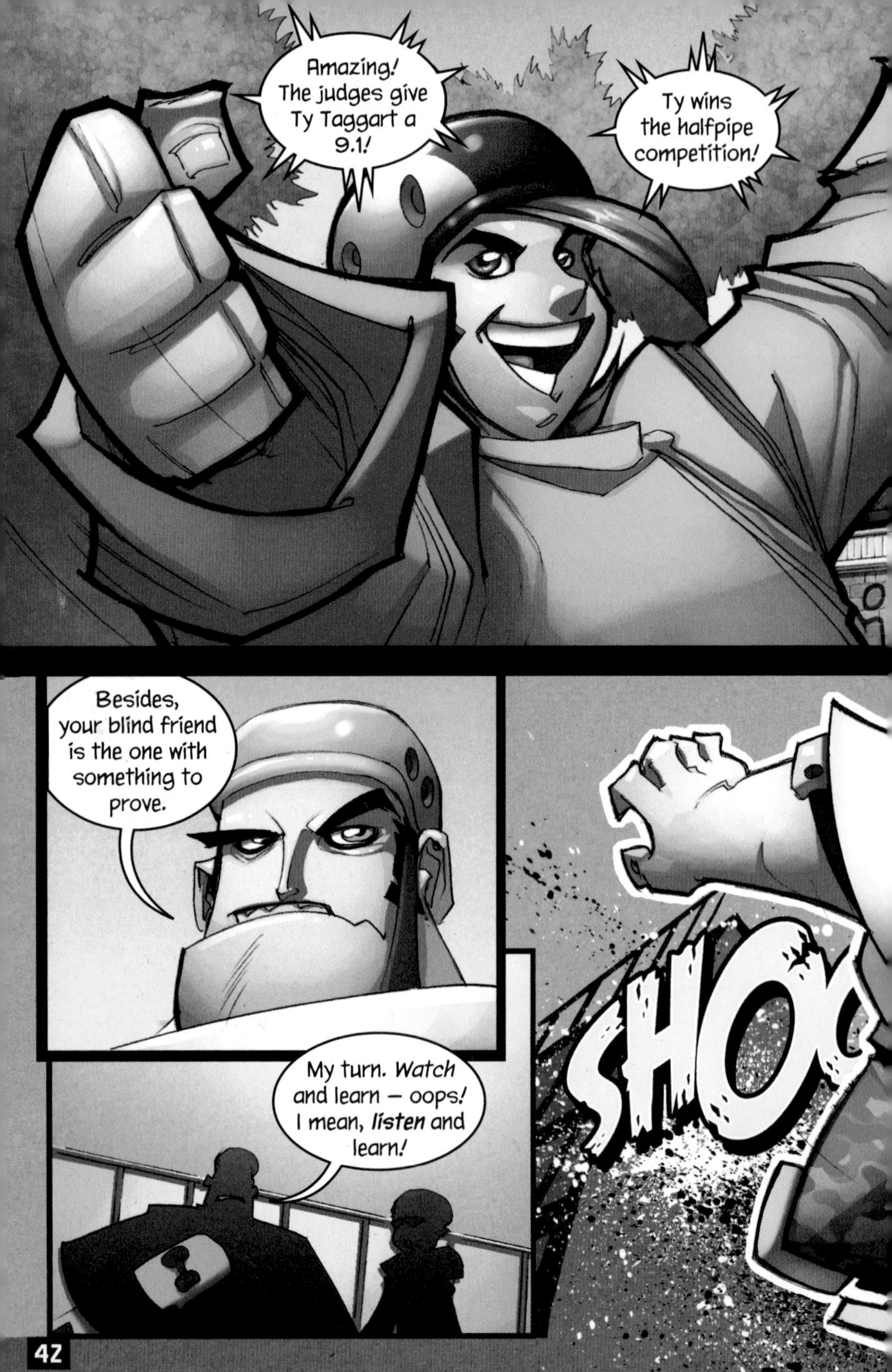
Amazing! The judges give Ty Taggart a 9.1!
Ty wins the halfpipe competition!
Besides, your blind friend is the one with something to prove.
My turn. *Watch* and learn — oops! I mean, ***listen*** and learn!
SHOO

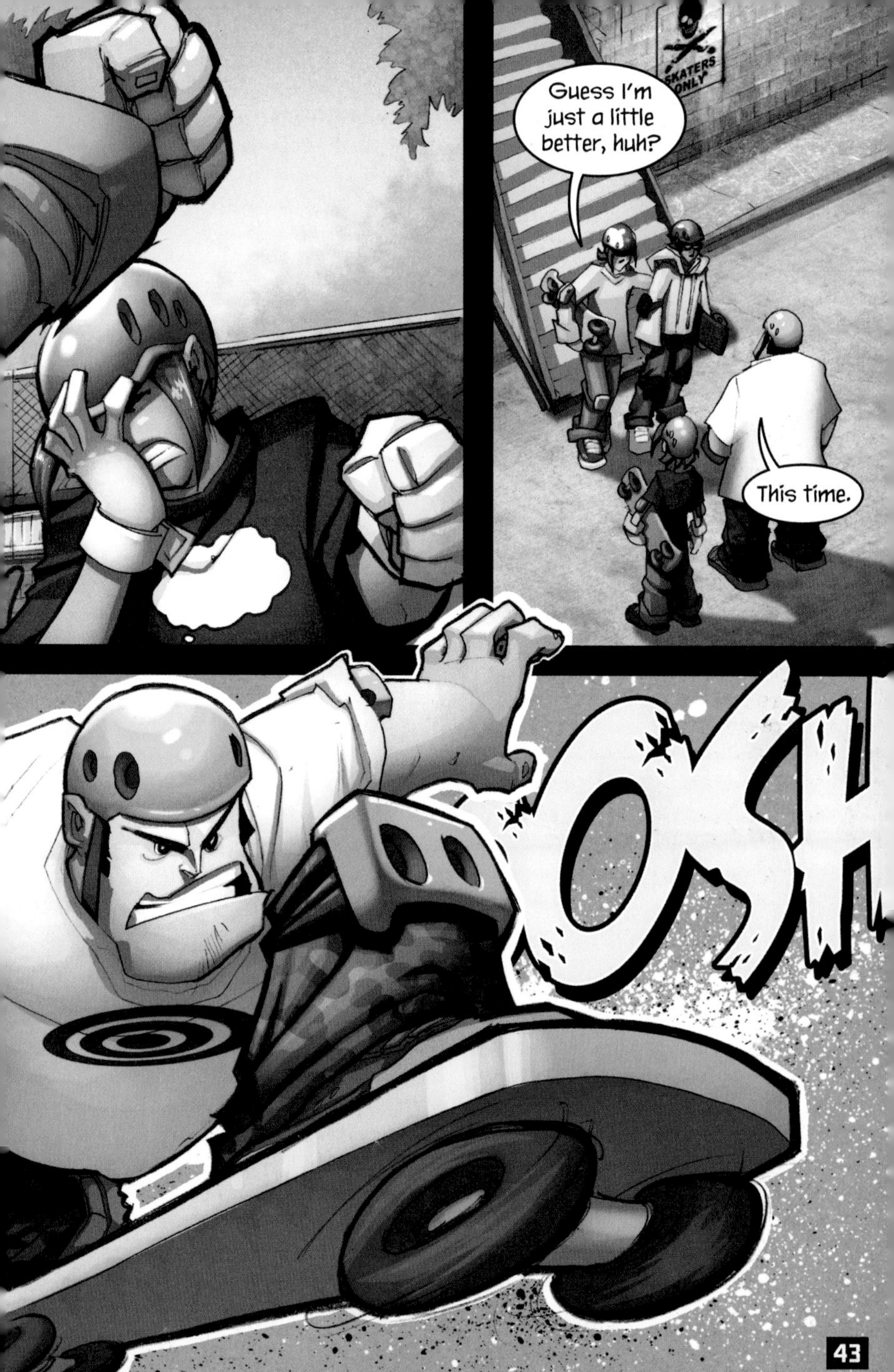

SKATERS ONLY
Guess I'm just a little better, huh?
This time.
OSH

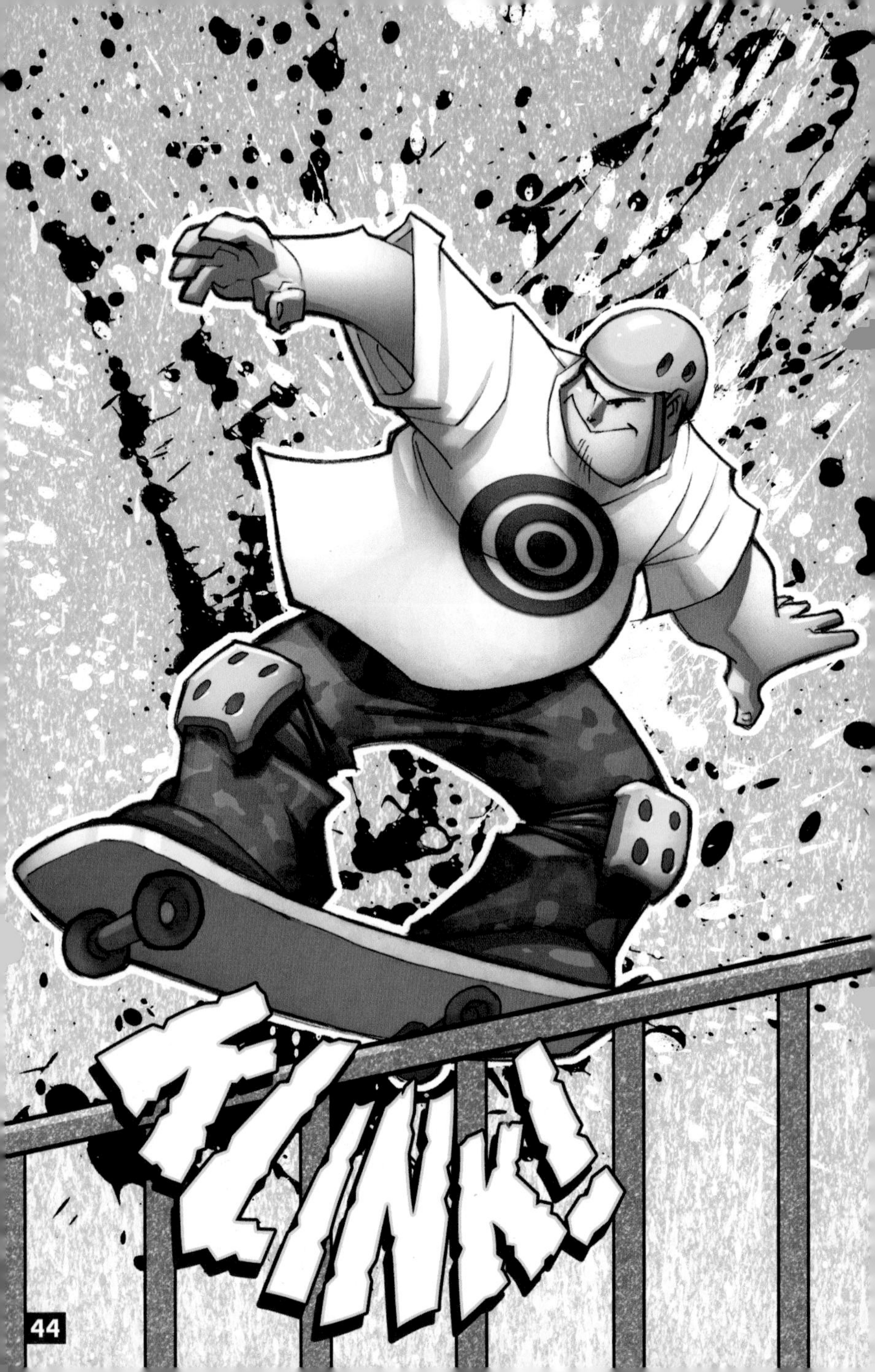
ZINK!

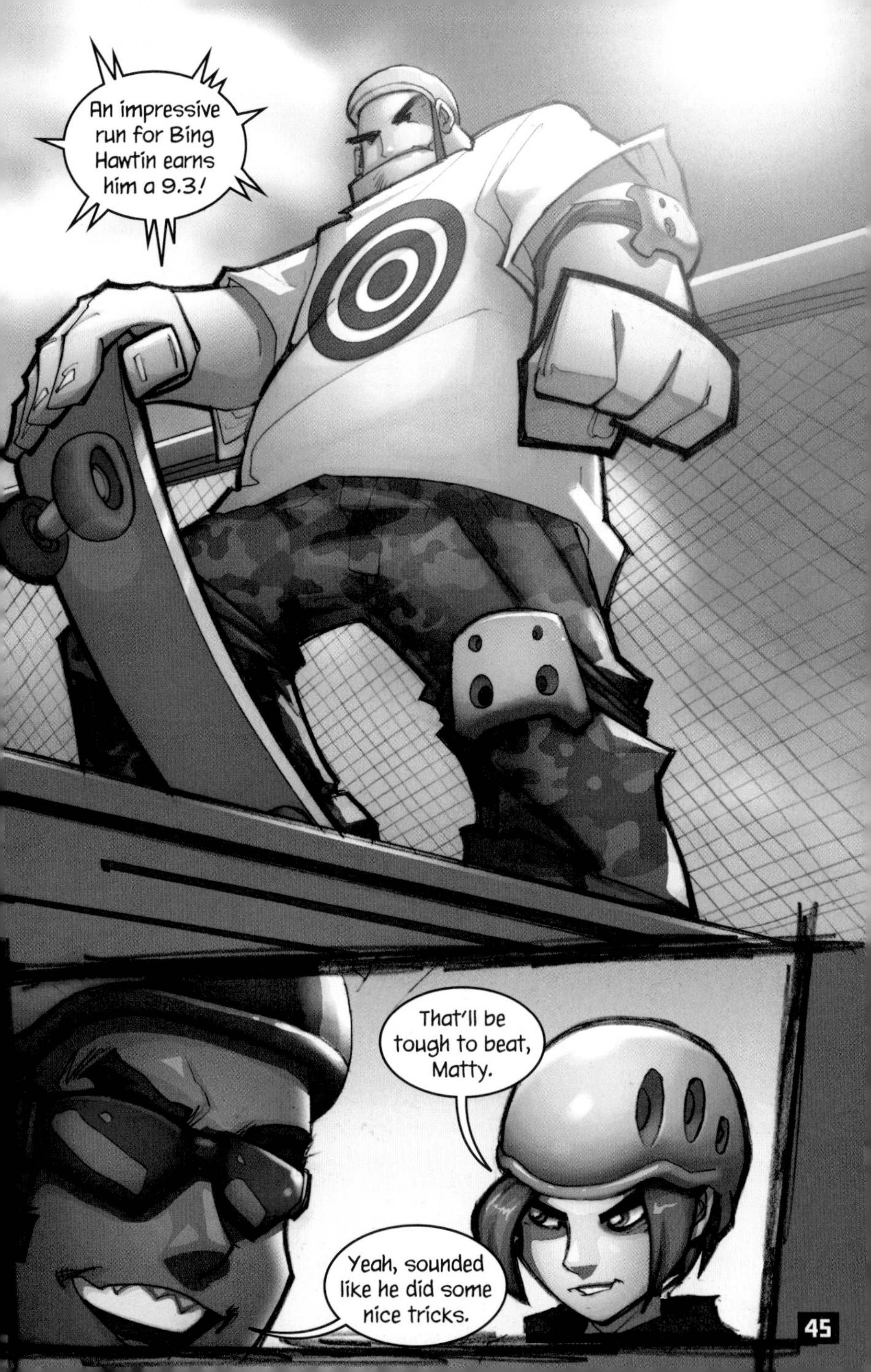
An impressive run for Bing Hawtin earns him a 9.3!
That'll be tough to beat, Matty.
Yeah, sounded like he did some nice tricks.

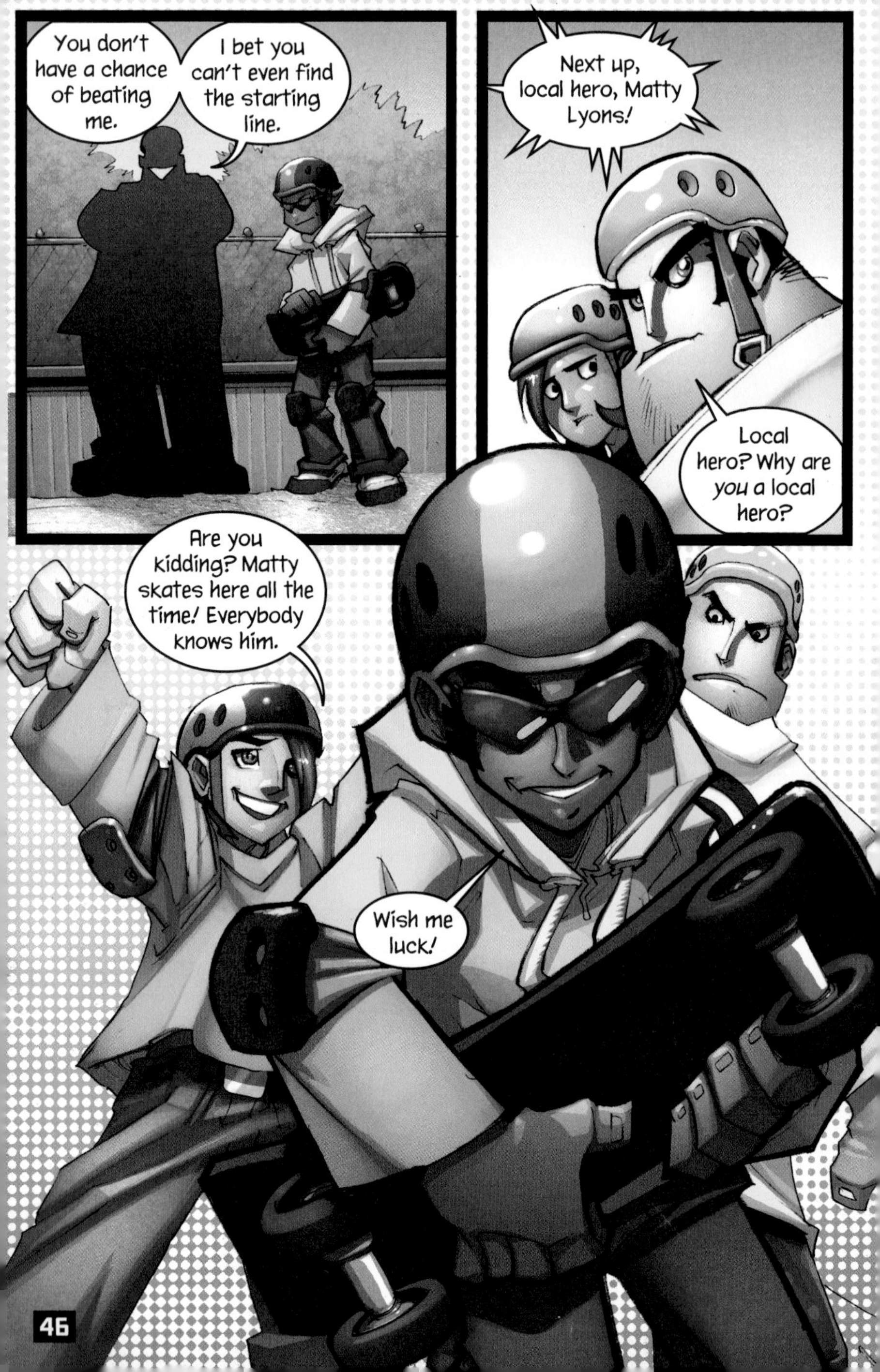
You don't have a chance of beating me.
I bet you can't even find the starting line.
Next up, local hero, Matty Lyons!
Local hero? Why are you a local hero?
Are you kidding? Matty skates here all the time! Everybody knows him.
Wish me luck!

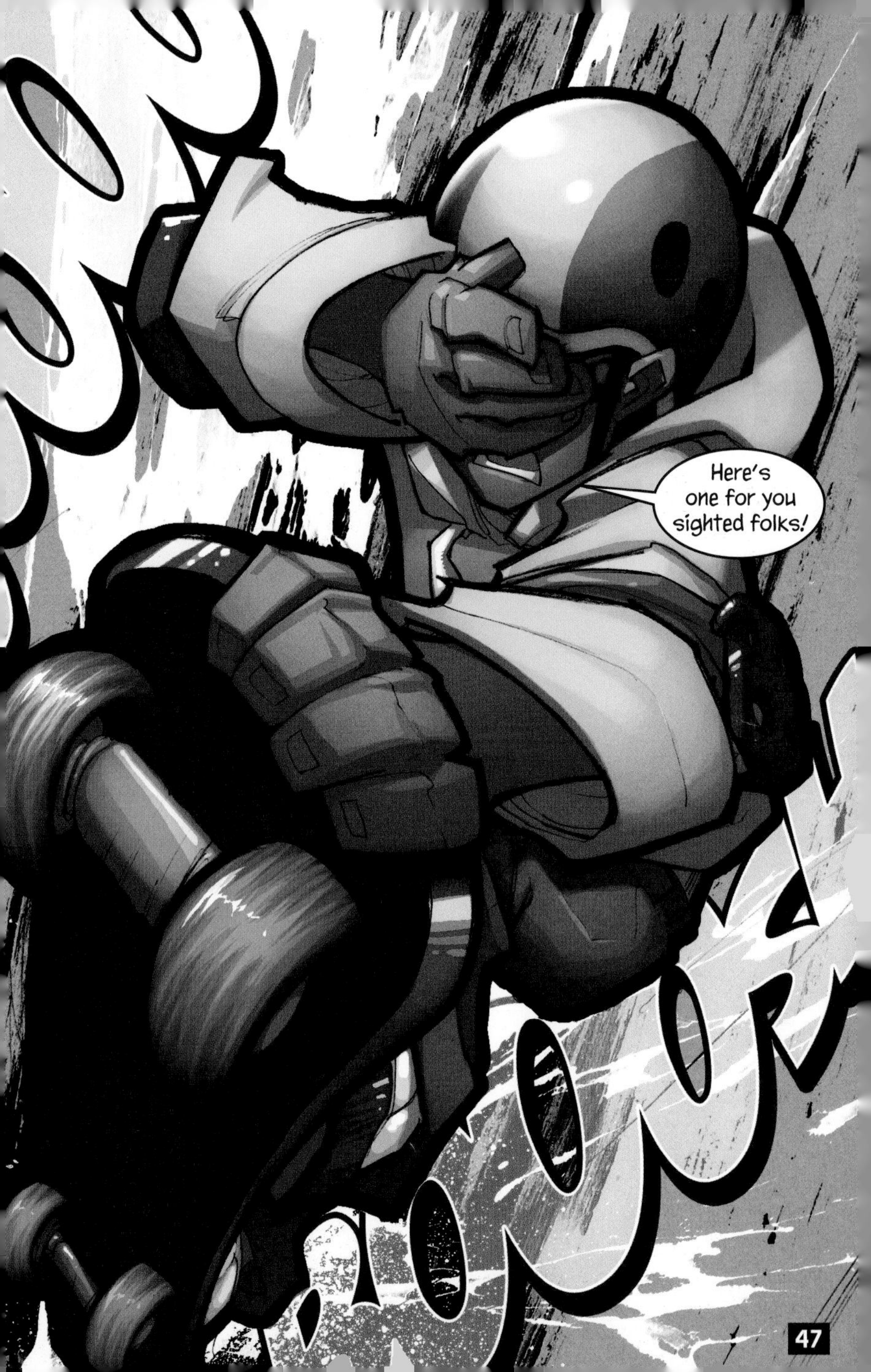
Here's one for you sighted folks!

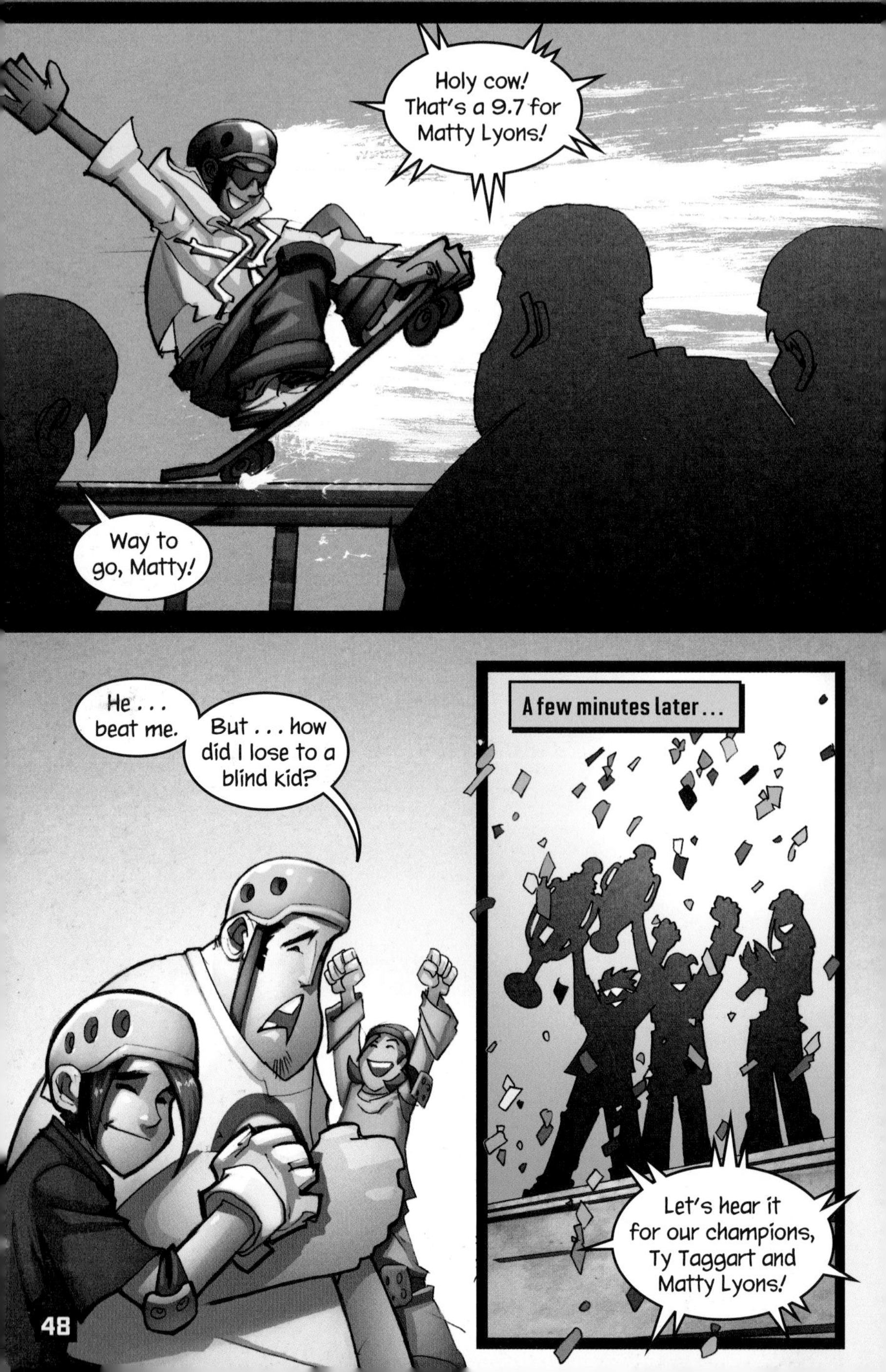
Holy cow! That's a 9.7 for Matty Lyons!
Way to go, Matty!
He . . . beat me.
But . . . how did I lose to a blind kid?
A few minutes later . . .
Let's hear it for our champions, Ty Taggart and Matty Lyons!

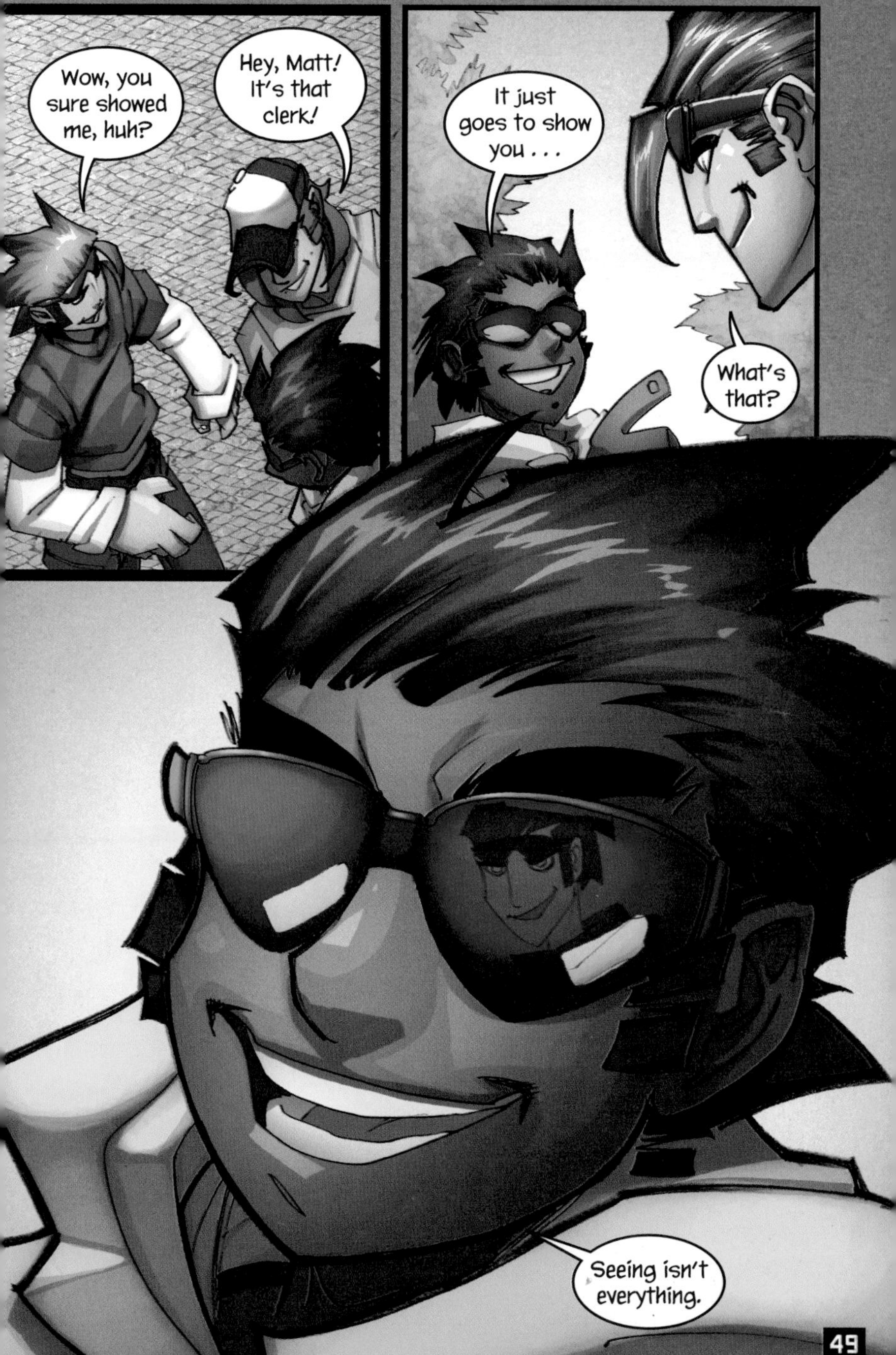
Wow, you sure showed me, huh?
Hey, Matt! It's that clerk!
It just goes to show you . . .
What's that?
Seeing isn't everything.

PORTS ZONE

STGAME RECAP

KT

ARDING

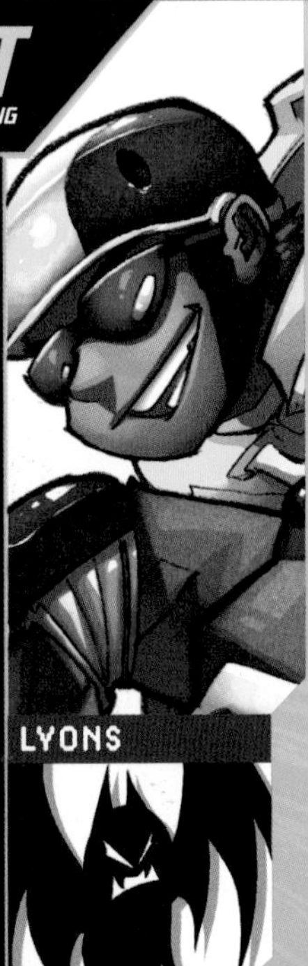
LYONS

BLIND SKATER BEATS BULLY BOARDER ON THE STREET COURSE!

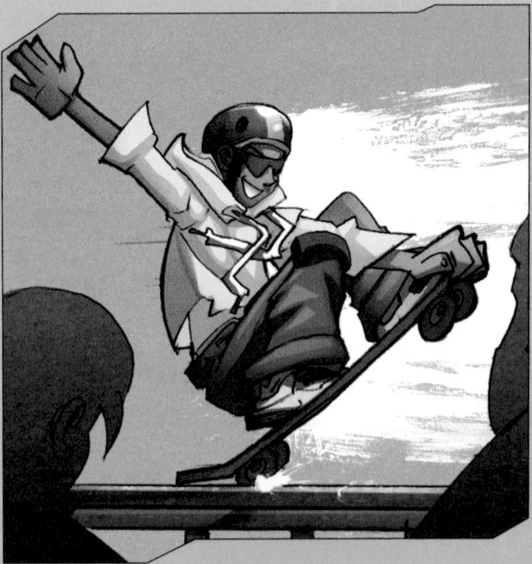

Y THE UMBERS

REET COURSE:
ATTY: 9.0, 9.7
NG: 9.1, 9.3

ALFPIPE:
: 8.8, 9.1
INT: 8.9, 8.9

STORY: Six-time street course champion, Bing Hawtin, finally met his match earlier today when blind skater, Matthew Lyons, took home the All-City trophy. Matty earned many new fans in his two routines for his creativity and technical skill. When asked how he felt about being a blind skater, Matt was quoted as saying that "seeing isn't everything."

Sports Illustrated KIDS

UP NEXT: SI KIDS INFO CENTER

POWERED BY **STONE ARCH**

BLZ vs BHS
3-1
TGR vs RDR
33-32
EAG vs BAN
14-7
SPA vs WLD
4-3
BAN vs RDR
21-15
RDR vs LIG
4-3
BLZ vs BHS

SZ POSTGAME *EXTRA*

WHERE *YOU* ANALYZE THE GAME!

Skateboarding fans got a real treat today when Matty one-upped runner-up, Bing Hawtin, on the street course. Let's go into the stands and ask some fans for their opinions on the day's events ...

DISCUSSION QUESTION 1

Matty is blind, but he didn't let his disability prevent him from skateboarding. If you were blind, how would your life be different? How would it be the same?

DISCUSSION QUESTION 2

Ty Taggart had some trouble managing his anger. What do you do when you get angry? Can anger ever be a good thing? Why or why not?

WRITING PROMPT 1

Bing the bully is out to get Matt and Ty. Have you ever had to deal with a bully? What happened? Write about your bully experience.

WRITING PROMPT 2

Matty and Ty win the street course and halfpipe competitions, respectively. Have you ever competed for something? What happened? Write about it.

(AIR)—if you grab air, you are riding with all four skateboard wheels off the ground

(KON-duhkt)—behavior

(ek-oh-loh-KAY-shuhn)—the method of locating something by determining the time for an echo to return to its source, like with radar or sonar

(GRAB)—if you perform a grab, you hold on to your skateboard and strike a pose in midair

(GRINDE)—if you do a grind, you skate with one or both axles of your board on a curb, railing, or other surface

(HAF-pipe)—a U-shaped ramp of any size, usually with a flat section in the middle, that is used for skateboarding

(SY-tid)—if you are sighted, then you are able to see. Sighted is the opposite of blind.

(uhn-SPORTS-muhn-like)—not displaying the behavior of a good sport, or to play dirty

CREATORS

ERIC STEVENS › *Author*

Eric Stevens lives in St. Paul, Minnesota. He is studying to become a middle-school English teacher. His favorite things include pizza, video games, watching cooking shows on TV, riding his bike, and trying new restaurants. Some of his least favorite things include olives and shoveling snow.

GERARDO SANDOVAL › *Illustrator*

Gerardo Sandoval is a professional comic book illustrator from Mexico. He has worked on many well-known comics including the Tomb Raider books from Top Cow Productions. He has also worked on designs for posters and card sets.

BENNY FUENTES › *Colorist*

Benny Fuentes lives in Villahermosa, Tabasco in Mexico, where it's just as hot as the sauce is. He studied graphic design in college, but now he works as a full-time colorist in the comic book industry for companies like Marvel, DC Comics, and Top Cow Productions. He shares his home with two crazy cats, Chelo and Kitty, who act like they own the place.

Sports Illustrated KIDS GRAPHIC NOVELS

QUICK COMIC

NOAH AND PETER ELLLESTON IN:

POINT-BLANK PAINTBALL

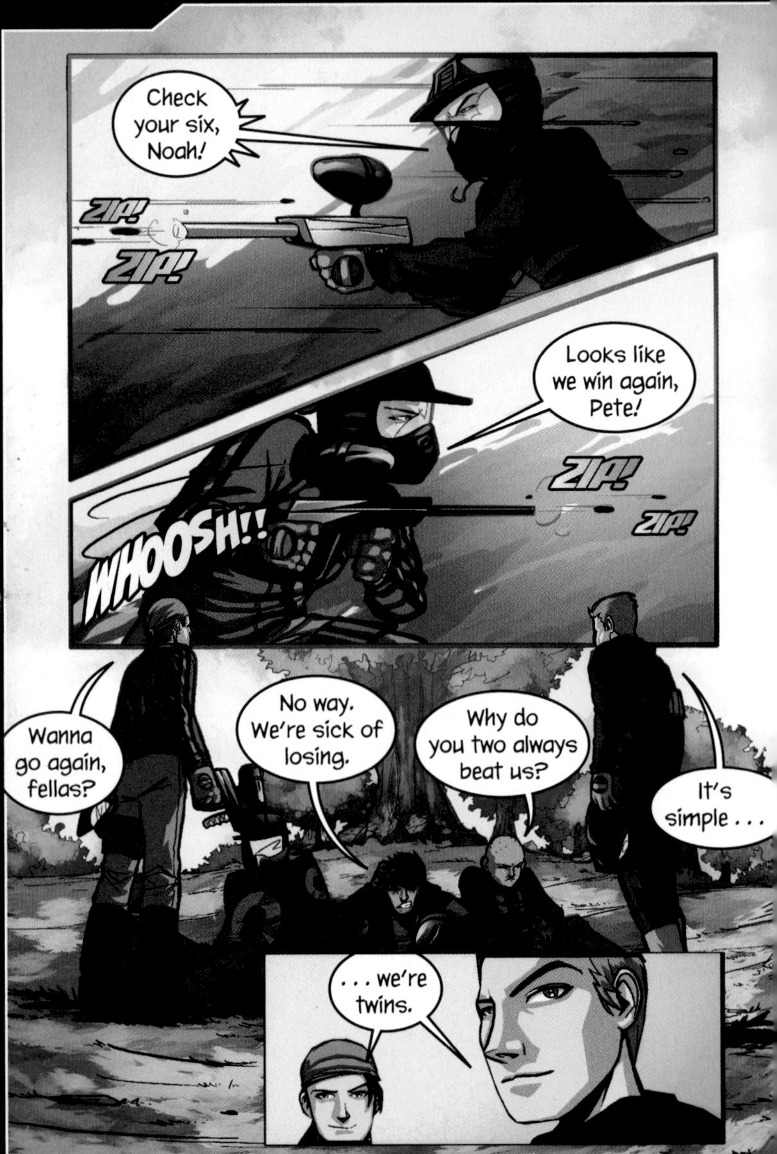

Check your six, Noah!
ZIP!
ZIP!
Looks like we win again, Pete!
ZIP!
ZIP!
WHOOSH!!
Wanna go again, fellas?
No way. We're sick of losing.
Why do you two always beat us?
It's simple . . .
. . . we're twins.

» LOVE THIS QUICK COMIC? READ THE WHOLE STORY IN POINT-BLANK PAINTBALL – ONLY FROM STONE ARCH BOOKS!

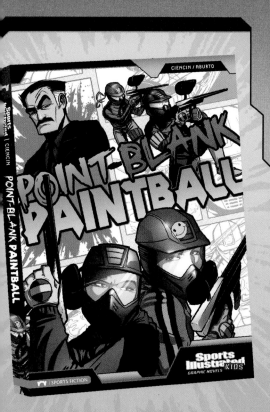

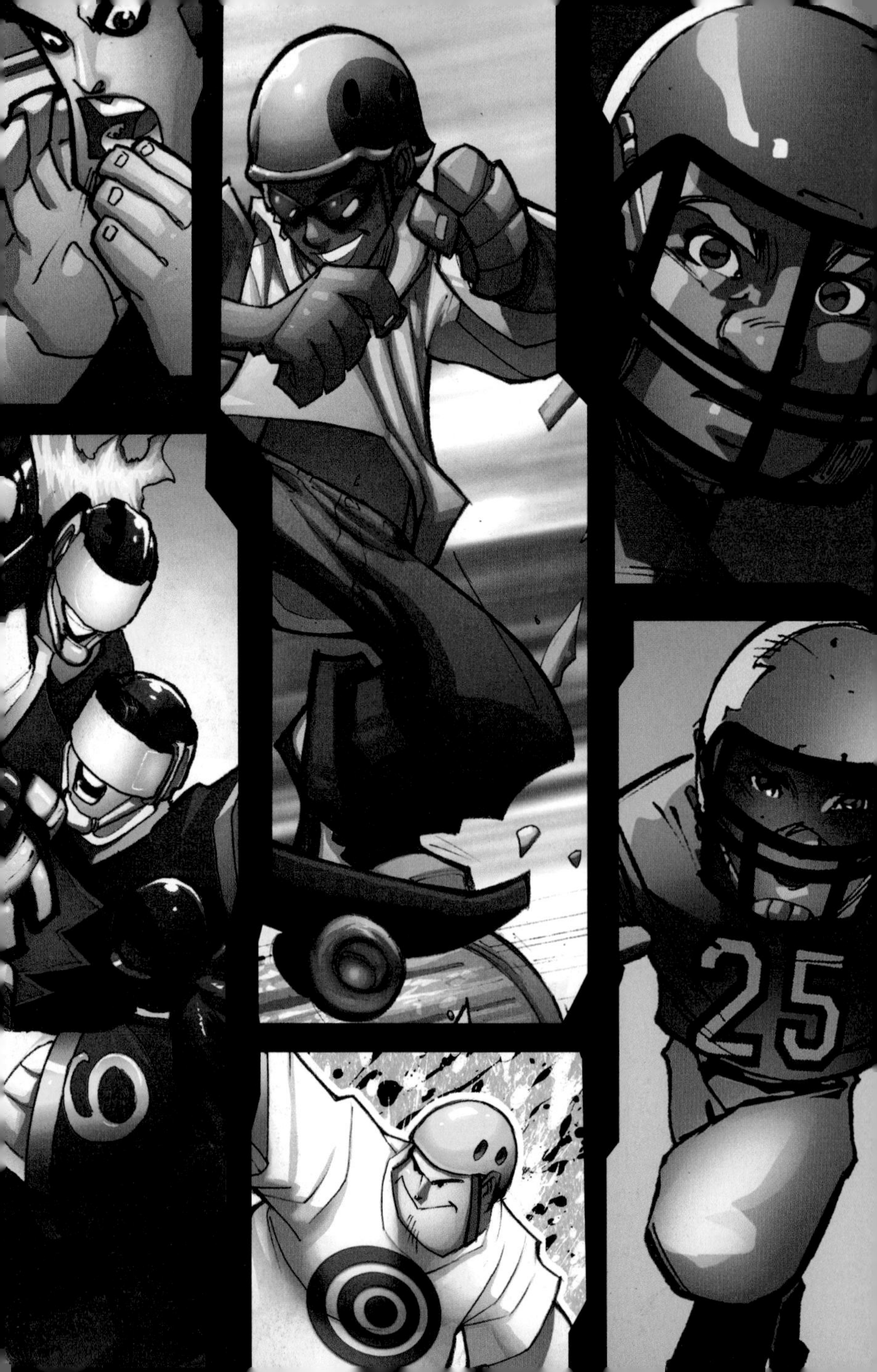
25

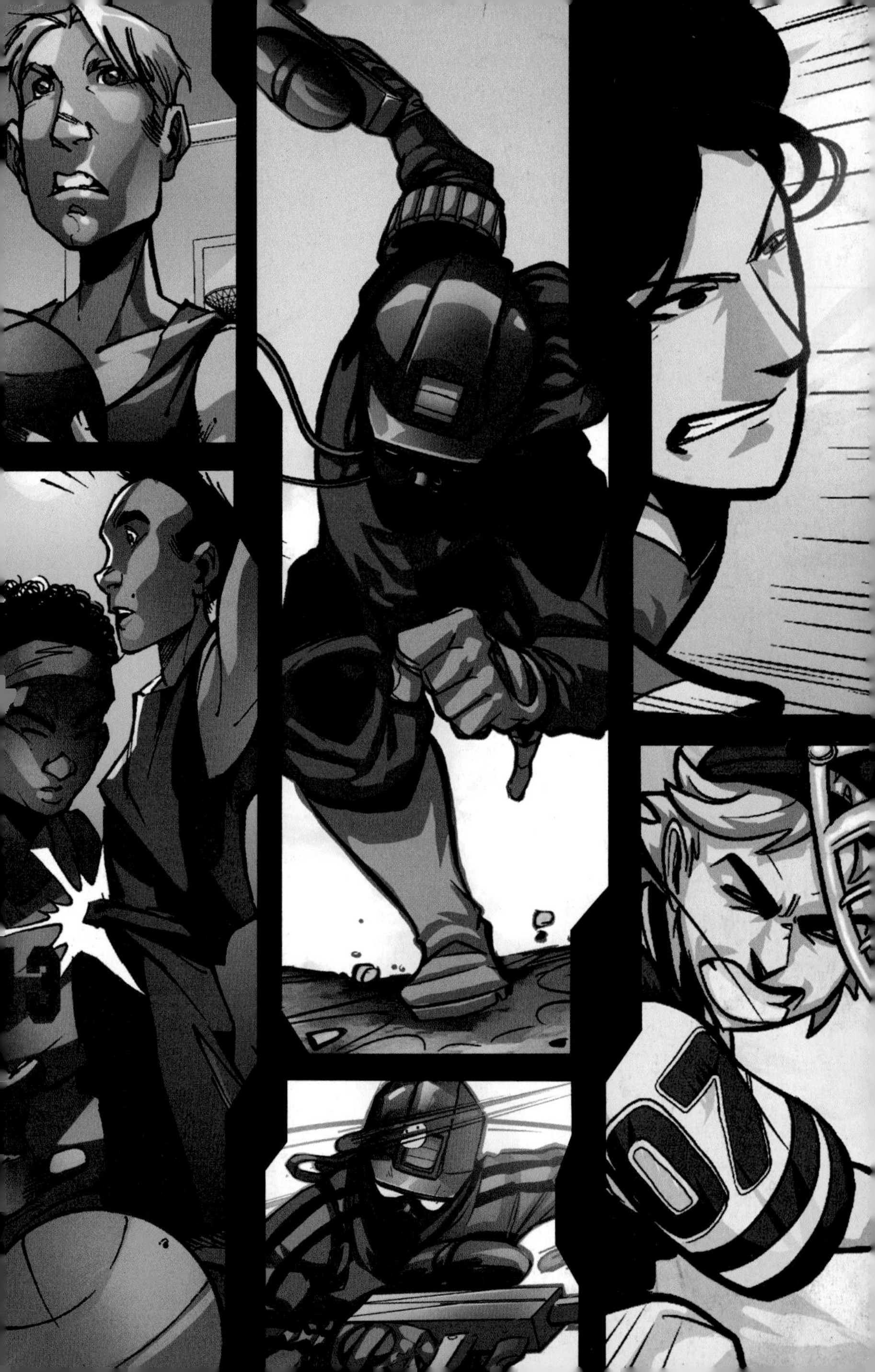

Sports Illustrated KIDS
GRAPHIC NOVELS

STONE ARCH BOOKS
a capstone imprint